# UNREVEALED

I0601412

## FOUR JANE PERRY STORIES

# LAUREL
# DEWEY

THE
STORY PLANT

The Story Plant
The Aronica-Miller Publishing Project, LLC
P.O. Box 4331
Stamford, CT 06907

Cover design by Barbara Aronica-Buck
Author photo by Carol Craven

Print ISBN-13: 978-1-61188-023-6
E-book ISBN: 978-1-61188-024-3

Visit our website at www.thestoryplant.com

First Story Plant Paperback Printing: October 2011

# TABLE OF CONTENTS

# ANONYMOUS

My name is Jane Perry and I'm an alcoholic.

As I write that, it doesn't feel like it belongs to me yet. I'm three months sober, so I'll get another goddamn chip at the meeting tomorrow night. Can't wait. The fucking thing can rattle around in the left pocket of my jeans and keep the other chips company.

This whole sobriety trip is still like a new shoe — too constrictive and rubbing my sole the wrong way. But I play along, go to the Alcoholics Anonymous meetings, listen to the Basement People (as I call them) talk, and convince myself that I am powerless over alcohol and my life has become unmanageable. That's the first step in AA, and it took me more than twenty years to make that leap.

But I also fight the notion that there are some alcoholics who really *should* tap a keg because they suck at sobriety. They are the ones who are wound so fucking tight that the least amount of stress kicks them into a frenzied orbit. That's when they're told to meditate or do yoga or take a long walk or breathe deeply. But the fact of the matter is, they really just need to get a load on, and it's just too fucking bad they can't stop popping a cap after one or two beverages.

Some nights, when I'm lying awake, I wonder if I'm one of those people who shouldn't be a teetotaler. But then I remember that there's no way I could stop at two beers or two shots of Jack Daniels. Hell, two drinks was a warm-up for me. I didn't get my drink on officially until I hit *numero* six. In AA, you have to delve into *why* you drink and what triggers the need to disappear. I find it ironic that a group dedicated to uncovering the need to disappear has the word *anonymous* in its title. Shouldn't they call it Alcoholics Identified? When you lay it on the table and really start pulling the layers off that goddamn onion, you discover that those of us who like to bend our elbows are really just wishing we could escape and become someone else—and we believe that if we became that someone else, the problems wouldn't follow us. But then every time you go to a meeting, you're reminded that the voices and the nightmares follow you no matter how radically you reinvent yourself.

I thought I was ready to reinvent myself after working my last case at Denver Homicide. I had nothing left in me. My adrenal glands had coughed up their last teaspoon of adrenaline. My world had turned on its ass, and I was forced to understand that there's more to heaven and earth than we can perceive. I couldn't digest everything that had happened, and so when my boss, Sergeant Morgan Weyler, offered me the job of sergeant working next to him, I knew I wasn't ready to deal with it. But I still had to be a cop because I came out of the womb with a desire to solve crimes and to understand why people do evil deeds.

So, like I said, I reinvented myself and started my own PI agency, called JPI for Jane Perry Investigations. I've had the shingle out for a little less than a month, and I'm catching a few cases that don't deal with dead bodies. The press I got after the Lawrence murder case helped get my name out there. My reluctant appearance on Larry King's show still earns me free coffees at the Gourmet Grind. Even though I hated doing it, it was a necessary evil. So when I went from Detective Jane Perry at Denver Homicide to Jane Perry, Private Investigator, I hoped that all those shadows that haunted me as a Denver cop would disappear and I could be reborn and start fresh.

That all dovetails with the case I worked this week. The fallout still has me smoking more than my normal pack a day.

It started last Monday night, when I was sitting with the Basement People at the Methodist church. During the break, I went outside to smoke and this woman, who I thought was around fifty, sidled up to me.

"You're Jane Perry, right?" she said, taking a hard suck of nicotine off her cigarette.

"Jane P.," I corrected her. "Remember where we are?"

"Yeah, yeah," she muttered, not giving a shit about anonymous protocol. "My name's Ellen Brigham. I saw you on Larry King's show."

"Who the fuck didn't?" I said, hoping to God she wasn't going to ask me to sign a copy of the group members' phone list.

Ellen went on to say that she'd heard I'd opened up my own PI office and wanted to know what I charged. I took one look at her shredded jeans, faded T-shirt and dirty tennis shoes and figured she couldn't afford even half of my usual $175 an hour plus expenses.

Without answering her question, I asked another. "What do you need?"

"I was wondering if you can find dead people?"

"Sure," I said, taking a hit off my cigarette. "I just go to any morgue or cemetery and there they are. Dead people."

"I should rephrase that," Ellen said, struggling with her thoughts. "My older sister, Marge Challis, she was last heard from back in the fall of 2001."

I dropped my cigarette to the pavement and snuffed it out with the toe of my cowboy boot. "I need a lot more than that."

"Like what?"

"Like her last known location and the date she went missing."

"That's easy. She was in tower number one on 9/11."

Well, that got my attention. I agreed to meet Ellen at my office the next day. She showed up early, dressed almost exactly the way she'd been outside the meeting. She said she'd taken the bus and walked five blocks to my office. She looked like she'd come right out of the homeless shelter. Her gray-streaked brown hair was half-combed and her face appeared haggard. I hadn't noticed the brown mole at the right corner of her bottom lip the night before.

After sitting down across from me, Ellen removed a large blue binder from her cloth bag. She was quick to apologize for her unkempt appearance, telling me she hadn't slept a wink the night before. It had taken her six years to get the guts to talk to somebody.

"Can I smoke in here?"

"Denver building code says no. I say why the fuck not?" Ellen nervously rummaged through her bag, coming up empty-handed. After about a minute, I handed her a pack of Marlboros. Ellen took a cigarette out and handed the pack back to me. "Keep 'em. So, what's the story?"

Ellen lit up, took a meaningful drag and gathered her thoughts. "Her name is Marge Challis."

"Is?" I questioned.

Ellen tilted her head. She struggled with the concept. "Was."

"Challis her married name or —"

"No, she never married." Ellen spelled the last name out for me so I could make a note.

"So, your last name of Brigham is —"

"I got married young and divorced. But I kept his name...."

I noticed how Ellen's voice inflected upward right then. It could be the sign of a lie but it could have also been nerves.

"Marge was having trouble back then."

"What kind of trouble?" I asked.

"Emotional and financial." Ellen looked me in the eye straight on for the first time. "She had a 9:00 a.m. job interview for a secretarial position in tower one. If she didn't get the job, she was basically gonna be kicked out of her apartment. She was drowning in credit card debt. Life had become unlivable."

I noticed that when Ellen talked about her sister, she seemed to have an outstanding grasp of what her sister had gone through.

Ellen continued. "Marge always wanted to be successful. Marry the good guy, live in the nice house, maybe have a kid. But deep down she never thought she was good enough to deserve any of that." Ellen took a deep drag on her cigarette. "This is real hard for me."

"Take your time."

"She got involved in drugs." Ellen looked ashamed. "Ecstasy and pills. She did meth for a while. That fucked her up."

"How old was she in the fall of 2001?"

"Twenty-eight."

"Twenty-eight?" I questioned.

"Yeah."

"So, she'd be thirty-four now?"

"Yeah. That's right."

"And she's your *older* sister?"

Ellen shrugged. "Yeah. What's the problem?"

The woman sitting across from me looked fifty. Her face was gaunt and aging rapidly. The gray in her hair lent even more maturity. I wanted to be diplomatic but diplomacy has never been my forte. "How old are you?"

Ellen hesitated slightly. "Thirty-three."

*Good God*, I thought. Talk about rode hard and put away wet. I thought I looked like shit for thirty-five, but the woman sitting across from me had obviously experienced one helluva stressful life to look that bad at thirty-three. "You're thirty-three?" I said, just to make sure my hearing wasn't going.

She could see that I was confused. "Marge and I are Irish twins," Ellen offered, using the term for siblings born less than twelve months apart.

"Any other siblings?"

Ellen's eyes welled with tears. "There was a brother. Frank. He was really good to Marge. He gave her money when she was broke and never expected it to be paid back. He'd talk to her any hour of the day or night for as long as she needed to talk. He'd tell her to keep positive and that she deserved a better life."

"He died?"

Ellen's eyes scanned the carpet. She took another drag on her cigarette. "Yeah. Right after 9/11. Car crash."

The first thing I thought was, what were the odds of losing two siblings in that short a period? The second thought was how tragic life could be. Jesus, no wonder Ellen was a drunk. "You say Frank was good to Marge. Was he good to you?"

"What?" She seemed unprepared for that question.

"We all need a decent person to talk to who actually gives a shit. Did Frank give you the same pep talks he gave your older sister?"

"Well, sure…uh, yeah. He was a good guy." Ellen appeared flustered. "I'm not trying to say he didn't help me. He *did*. But we're not here to talk about me. We're here to talk about Marge and the possibility of…"

I sensed a lot of nerves kicking in right then. I leaned forward, clasping my hands on my cluttered desk. "Of what?"

"That maybe she didn't die." The words fell like stone. Ellen pulled her large blue binder to her lap, opened it and rifled through a disorganized heap of pages. "She was on the sixteenth floor. Her interview was with a bank." Ellen found the page she was looking for. "The plane struck tower one at 8:46 a.m. It hit floors ninety-three to ninety-nine. No one above those floors survived. Below the crash line, approximately seventy-two die but over *four thousand* survive! Tower one doesn't collapse until 10:28 a.m. Being on the sixteenth floor, even if the elevators didn't work, she could have walked down sixteen floors real quick —"

"How do you know all the details about your sister's schedule that day?"

Ellen looked taken aback. "Well, we talked." Her eyes drifted to the side. "We didn't talk a lot but I knew about her interview. She called me a few days before and told me about it." Ellen's chin quivered as her mouth went dry. This wasn't just nerves, I realized. This was outright fear. "You got some water?"

I grabbed the cleanest glass I could find and filled it with some bottled water. Ellen drank it like she'd just run a marathon in 110-degree heat.

I wanted to gauge my next question carefully. "Did she call you…from the tower?"

Ellen looked at me. "No. She called Frank."

"Not you."

"No. She called Frank." Ellen hung her head. "He told me what she said. She called him right after 10:00 a.m…. right after tower two collapsed. She told him how she saw the debris hit the windows, obscuring everything outside. And the way the ground shook, like bombs were goin' off all around her. And…how they should have evacuated right away but she was scared." Ellen's hand trembled. "She told him she wasn't sure if she'd get out alive. And that she loved him. That he'd been the only good thing in her life. And that this was a sign from God."

There must have been some serious rift between Ellen and her sister, I thought, for Marge to say that Frank was the "only good thing" in her life. "Wait a second," I said. "She had twenty-five minutes or so from when she called Frank to get out safely and walk down sixteen floors —"

"Maybe she figured she wasn't worth saving." Ellen seemed to be in another world.

I sat back. "What are you saying? She made a split decision to commit suicide in the tower?"

Ellen was silent for almost a minute. "Her life was so messed up. Maybe she decided at that moment that Marge Challis needed to die."

I watched Ellen's face fight the words she just said. But I also knew that even when people say they don't want to live, it doesn't necessarily mean they want to die. The will to survive is programmed into our DNA. I knew from my own dark past that just because I'd wanted to check out a few times, it didn't mean that the driving force to sustain my life hadn't taken over. You may hate life but you may fear death even more.

"So, she tells Frank that the terror attack is a sign from God and then what?" I asked.

Ellen's eyes filled with tears. "She told him she loved him and that she had to make a difficult decision."

"To live or die."

Ellen nodded weakly.

"Then what?"

"She hung up. And no one ever heard from Marge after that."

"Ellen," I said cautiously, "I don't mean to be insensitive. But why are you here?"

"I needed you to hear my story. We're anonymous at the meetings. But I wanted you to know about me and what happened to Marge. I've never told anyone about it."

"You're kidding."

"I'm not. They tell us at AA to make amends for past wrongs. To face people you've hurt and let them know that you weren't thinking clearly when you were using and that," she choked on her tears, "that I shouldn't have let Marge die."

"But you didn't have any control over that. Marge called Frank from the tower. Not you."

"What I mean is I should have helped her more. I should have believed in her more. I should have filled her up with hope instead of..." Her thoughts drifted.

"Instead of what?"

"Making her think she wasn't worth saving!"

And that, I decided, was why Ellen looked like she was fifty. She and her sister obviously had a falling-out, with probably minimal contact toward the end of Marge's life. Although, I recalled, Ellen said she did talk to her a few days prior to the job interview. I ruminated on it and deduced that the inevitable guilt and all the what-if's had flooded Ellen's head for six painful years. At that moment, I realized that Ellen wasn't talking to me because she needed a PI. Ellen needed someone to confess to. I was a priest and Ellen was confessing her sins. I took a breath and did my best to assume the role. "So, if Marge was alive today, what do you think she'd be doing?"

Ellen looked at me with soulful eyes. "She'd be clean and sober. I'd make sure of that. She'd still be searching but she'd be trying to get her life together. She'd be…reaching out to people, like I'm reaching out to you." Ellen considered the question further. "Frank wouldn't be dead either."

"How's that possible? He died in a car crash."

Ellen's gaze moved from me to the side. "Well, after Marge died, Frank got preoccupied a lot. His mind wandered and, well, her death impacted him. I'm sure that's why he wasn't paying attention when he slid on the ice."

"Where'd he live?"

"Vermont." Ellen smiled at a pleasant memory. "He was an *award-winning photographer*." She said that to me almost like she wanted to make damn sure I heard her. Tears welled in her eyes. "So, if Frank wasn't dead and Marge was alive and clean and sober, I know he would be so proud of her. *So* proud. And he'd know that all those late-night phone calls with her finally paid off and that she was figuring out that she *did* deserve to have a good life." Ellen looked at me with near desperation. "I wish to God Frank could know that, Jane. It'd mean the world to me."

"If there's a heaven, Ellen, then they're together and he knows how much he helped Marge." Shit, now I really *did* sound like a goddamn priest.

"Right," she whispered, as if she didn't believe that Marge and Frank were shooting the breeze in the afterlife. "I just wish..."

"What?"

She shook her head and shrugged her shoulders. "I just wish."

It was an odd statement, but I let it go. Ellen closed the blue binder and put it back in her bag. "Thank you for listening to me." She squashed out the spent cigarette in my ashtray.

"Sure."

"What do I owe you?"

"Nothing."

Ellen looked a bit shocked. "Wow. Thank you." She got up and walked toward the door, let out a nervous long breath and then turned back to me. "What if she got out? What if she walked away from the towers and kept walking? What if she's out there, scared to death and wishing she could make everything right?"

Ellen sounded delusional at that point. But I was also sure that the same thought had crossed the minds of others who lost family on 9/11, since they never saw their loved one's body and had closure. For them and for Ellen, there was the comforting fantasy that somehow their nearest and dearest were out there, lost but alive.

She stared at me, and it seemed she was trying to get me to understand something with her mournful gaze. But all I could see then was regret and sorrow.

I couldn't shake Ellen's visit for five days. There was something about her that haunted me. I picked up the AA member phone list once with the idea of calling her but she wasn't on it. Maybe she didn't have a phone, although that would complicate her life when she had to reach her sponsor. But sponsors certainly weren't mandatory. I didn't have one. I figured by the looks of her, she was probably so broke that she didn't own a cell phone.

By Sunday afternoon, I was obsessed with Ellen's story. I thought about the tragedy of losing both her sister and brother so close together and I understood why she chose to disappear into a bottle. I wondered, briefly, if the story of the brother and sister's death might have made it to some news show. I'd seen plenty of post-9/11 human interest stories on TV and in the newspaper — stories that followed victims' families and revealed everything from suicides to new relationships. Call it curiosity, but I opened my laptop and searched "Frank Challis photography Vermont" based on the limited information Ellen had given me. The very first website was "Frank Challis Photography" and mentioned "In Memoriam" in the brief description. I clicked on the link and read about Frank's work. There was a beautiful shot of Vermont in the wintertime. I looked closer at the photo and saw the copyright. It was 2007.

I went through photo after photo and found current dates on most of them. Finally, at the bottom of one page, it read, "To contact Frank directly..." and gave a number. If Frank was dead, he sure as hell took great photos from the grave.

My eyes drifted to the "In Memoriam" link at the top of one of the pages. I clicked on it. It loaded slowly. First I saw the name "Marge" and then "Challis" appear. The photo took longer to load. But once it did, I stared in stunned silence. It was Ellen.

Sure, she looked younger and fresher, but it was Ellen. There was the striking brown mole by the right side of her bottom lip and the same haircut, with less gray. Even entertaining the idea that she and her "sister" were Irish twins, the chance of both of them having a large mole in the same location was a billion to one.

"Fuck," I said out loud. Not so much angry as confused. I thought back on the conversation I'd had with her. Little by little, the jigsaw puzzle started to make sense. I had wondered why "Ellen" knew so much about Marge's private thoughts and — how an estranged sister was able to tell me what Marge was going through and how it was affecting her. When she described the phone call that Frank allegedly told her about, she was really telling me what *she* saw out that window of tower one and what *she* felt at that critical moment. And when she told me, regretfully, that she shouldn't have let Marge die, that she "should have helped her more," believed in her, and filled her with hope instead of making her believe she wasn't worth saving, the poor woman was actually talking about herself. The addict she used to be. The one Frank tried so desperately to help.

I think I understand why she killed off Frank in her head. Once she "killed" herself, she had to "kill" him as well to assuage the loneliness. If he weren't dead in her mind, she might get weak when she was drunk and call him up to hear him tell her that everything was all right and that she wasn't a bad person. But as each year passed, and Marge Challis remained on the 9/11 victim list, the chance to resurrect her "dead body" and come clean became more unfeasible. Even though that's what she wanted more than anything. After she got sober and the cobwebs cleared, she came face-to-face with herself. She didn't want to be "dead" anymore. So she reinvented herself, like we all do when we shake loose the shadows of addiction. She became Ellen Brigham, went to more meetings, and finally got the guts to approach me and partially reveal her stained soul. She was on step nine in AA: making direct amends to people, whenever possible, for past wrongs. The problem was, the "dead" can't make direct amends.

I played back the visit to its conclusion, and I remembered the look she gave me right before she left — the look that almost pleaded with me to read her mind. "*I just wish,*" she stated. It had seemed odd to me then but not now. I was pretty sure that what she wished more than anything was for Frank to know she was okay. Like it was up to me to be a good PI, put the pieces together, maybe contact him, and… what? What in the hell was I supposed to do? I couldn't call Frank out of the blue and drop that bomb on him. Fuck that shit. It's called *direct* amends for a reason, not amends via a third party who also happens to be a drunk. No. I'd talk to her first at the meeting. Somehow, we'd figure out how to make it all right.

So, right now, I'm sitting in my Mustang sucking down my twenty-second cigarette of the day and I'm about to go inside the Methodist church for the weekly meet-and-greet with the Basement People. I've been keeping an eye out for Ellen — I mean, Marge, but I haven't seen her. The meeting starts in five minutes, and I want to get a good seat close to the bad coffee and bowls of shitty hard candy.

I walk down into the basement and the mood is grim. There're a few people crying and shaking their heads. I walk over to Joe, the guy who runs the meeting. He's not looking great either.

"What's going on?" I ask him.

"Sad news. I got a call yesterday. Ellen B. died."

"Fuck," was all I could muster. "What happened?"

"Car accident."

"What?"

"She fell asleep at the wheel and ran off the road. Died on impact."

I felt the walls start to cave in around me. Marge took the bus to my office. She didn't own a car. "How did you find out Ellen died?"

"I got a call from her cousin," Joe offered. "She said she found my number on the members' phone list."

It suddenly made sense to me. "Right. Her cousin. Marge Challis?"

Joe nodded.

And so the cycle of life and death, reinvention and resurrection continue for Marge. I contemplated calling Frank, but I figured I'd need a stiff drink before I did that. To preserve my sobriety, I opted out.

Like I said, in AA, you have to delve into *why* you drink and what triggers your need to disappear. Once you stop killing the pain with the bottle, you're supposed to come alive and find out who you really are and why you choose to exist. But some of us...some of us choose to walk out of a burning building that is twenty-five minutes away from collapsing, and before we get to the end of the street where the debris isn't so thick and the smoke has cleared, we've become someone else. And we believe in our hearts that the long shadows that stand just behind us will magically disappear just like the person we slaughtered. But those damn shadows are as uncompromising as we chose to be when we believed we could kill the past. They grasp us even more relentlessly.

Somewhere out there right now, Marge Challis thinks she's again shaken off the darkness. But when she wakes up tomorrow, there will be a little less light to guide her.

# YOU CAN'T JUDGE A BOOK

# BY ITS COVER

I want to be up-front with everyone who is reading this. I had to be talked into writing it. You see, I'm a very private person, and I'm not someone who readily opens herself up to others. I've always been like that, ever since I was a kid. When somebody showed a passing interest in me or in my life, I'd wonder why he cared and what his true motive was. Chalk it up to having a hardcore cop for a father. I'm suspicious of people in general and more than a little cynical. But I bet any cop would tell you the same thing.

For those of you who don't know me, my name is Jane Perry and I'm a homicide detective here in Denver, Colorado. Technically, it's Sergeant Detective Jane Perry, but most people I know just call me Jane. Being a cop is all I know how to do, and I'm good at it. That's not arrogance, that's confidence. I am the job, as they say. If I were flipping burgers, my head would still be programmed as a cop. It's in my blood. My dad was a homicide cop, and his buddies considered him top-notch. I didn't follow in his footsteps to be like him. The last thing I want to be is like my father. I'm a homicide cop because I like to wrap my mind around the mysteries of why people kill other people. I like to get into the heads of the killers.

I like to run around inside the victims' heads even more. I can walk into a hot crime scene while the blood is still wet and death still hangs heavy in the air and I can hear the walls whisper their secrets. Sometimes I can hear the screams and pleas of the victims before they took their last breath. Not hear it like in my ear. It's more like hearing it in my gut.

God, I sound fucking nuts. But that's the only way I can describe it. It's not some kind of psychic shit. It's so much deeper than that. *I hear the dead with my gut.* Yes. And it consumes me. And, believe me, it's changed me inside forever.

My former boss, Sergeant Morgan Weyler, who I now work alongside since my promotion to sergeant, is the one who actually talked me into writing down this particularly strange story. He thought it would be "cathartic" for me, since I refuse to go to therapy and be psychoanalyzed by a woman who keeps a dog-eared, tear-stained, heavily underlined copy of Freud's biography in her bathroom resting precariously on the back of her mauve toilet.

The first and only time I met the woman, I was immediately turned off by her sparrow-like features, translucent, veined skin and weak jawbone. She talked so quietly that I had to lean well within her three-foot comfort range just to hear her. When she told me I needed to "explore my boundaries and process my authentic self," I wanted to cap her with a 9-millimeter plug. She "suggested" that I had "anger issues." I told her she didn't need a degree in psychology to figure that out. The guy at my corner coffeehouse who's twenty and still hasn't graduated from high school made that brilliant deduction during my first interaction with him. When I left her office, she said I was being too "judgmental" about her. Those types of women love that word, *judgmental*. What they don't realize is that when they tell someone that they are being judgmental, that's a *judgment*. But they can't hear that because the irony horn is blaring too loudly.

I tend to read people fairly quickly. You have to be able to size others up in my line of work — to separate the real victims from the liars. But I've been sizing up people's actions since I was small child. When you're abused as a kid, you learn that you better assess people and their possible actions quickly because if you don't, you're going to be on the receiving end of one helluva punch. So I became what some therapists call hyper-vigilant. Sometimes, I had to judge a violent situation within seconds of its erupting. So I spend a lot of time stepping back and observing people. I'm always on guard; always waiting for the proverbial shoe to drop. That's probably why I smoke. I think the nicotine takes the edge off but allows me to still focus.

One way I learned to read people was through their body language and voice tones. People's mannerisms and subtle voice alterations are massive "tells" in determining whether someone is being truthful with me. My dad, Dale Perry, taught me all about body language, and he was damn good at it. That is about the only good thing I can say about him because he also taught me how to be a great drunk, how to fear, how to hurt, how to hate, how to see life as continual struggle and how to never feel that I'm good enough. Jesus, now *I* sound like a damn victim and that's the last thing I want to be. I despise victims. Not victims of crimes…victims

of life. People who can't build a bridge and get over their in-
ner turmoil. I'm actually particularly drawn to people who've
had to walk the harder path and come out better or worse on
the other end. *Survivors.* Yeah, that's who I champion. Maybe
that's because I see myself in them. I have great empathy for
the survivors of this world because I know what it takes to
climb out of severe trauma and reach deep within your heart
and soul and resurrect yourself into a new reality.

My road to resurrection has been a long and strange
one. During that trip, I've encountered some — how can I
say this without sounding crazy? — otherworldly phenom-
ena that I can't explain but that have operated within my life
and the lives of those around me. Mostly, it's the bizarre synchronicities — coincidences — that defy logic. Sometimes,
I've experienced prophetic dreams or feelings that have ma-
terialized in the waking world. The first few times it happened, it scared the shit out of me. I attributed it to too much
booze. While the booze may have loosened me up to make
me open to the phenomenon, there was something else op-
erating outside of the bottle. I no longer fight it, because in
many ways, I've always allowed my intuition to guide me,
even on hard-to-solve homicide cases. So these days, when
I encounter the odd person or the odder circumstance that
borders on the unexplainable, I don't fight it. I don't try to
explain it, and I try to work with it instead of against it.

I can give you a great example, one that definitely feeds
into what I was mentioning earlier about feeling empathy for
the survivors. I drew the short straw at the office (which is
Denver Homicide, or simply DH) and was asked by Sergeant
Weyler to give a classroom career-day lecture at one of the
public middle schools here in Denver. If you knew me, you'd
know I am *not* the person to be sent out to a goddamn school

to talk to these annoying midgets about my job. But, like I said, I drew the short straw.

So I get to the school for my 2:00 p.m. appearance, and I'm greeted by the effusive female principal who chose to wear her red power suit and four-inch black heels that day. And here's me, in my denim jeans, cowboy boots, light blue poplin shirt and leather jacket. I felt like the dyke who came to dinner standing next to her. After she shook my hand with her firm grip, she leaned forward and sniffed the air around me.

"You smoke?" she asked me.

"Yes," I admitted, "but I won't pass them out to the kids."

She got that deer-in-the-headlights expression on her face, not sure if I was kidding. She suggested that I take off my jacket, hoping that would erase the scent of tobacco, but I assured her that the nicotine was deeply embedded in my cell structure and probably had penetrated my DNA, so it was useless to remove my jacket. I then moved my jacket just far enough to reveal my Glock, which I always keep in my shoulder holster when I'm on duty. I thought she was going to fall backward on her four-inch FMPs when she saw it. She asked me to remove my service weapon, but I was getting pretty pissed by this point and told her that if the Glock left the building, so did I. I was actually hoping she would take me up on that offer because I really didn't want to sit in front of a bunch of jacked-up munchkins and field questions from them.

Unfortunately, she asked me to follow her into a sixth-grade classroom, where I was met with thirty pairs of gawking eyes. She introduced me as "a *female* detective" from the Denver Police Department, which I certainly thought was obvious since I do have shoulder-length brown hair and enough of a chest to not create confusion as to my sexual identity. But this broad seemed to want to make sure the kiddies knew I was a woman who was *also* a cop. Boggles the mind, eh? I guess that's because *Cagney & Lacey* was way before their time.

I had just been asked to sit on a wooden stool in front of the class and start my talk (which I hadn't given any thought to) when another teacher entered the classroom accompanied by a kid who looked about fourteen. He was taller than the other dwarfs in the room, and he was dressed like a junior anarchist, complete with black trousers, combat boots, *Matrix* jacket and T-shirt that sported two words in red block type: Question Everything! A quick glance at the power-suited principal told me that she wasn't happy to see the kid joining the class. All the pint-size members of the classroom turned around to gawk at the kid, who returned their stares with a crooked smile and a raised eyebrow. Even though he was led to a seat in the rear, I could see that there was something wonky with his left eye. He looked like he'd been bashed around too many times and had suffered some sort of facial trauma.

Irritation filled the space around the principal, who clicked her heels across the vinyl floor toward me and spoke in a hushed tone she usually reserved for admonishing wayward students.

"Looks like we're having an unexpected extra member of the class today," she whispered as a low murmur rolled across the classroom from the pre-pubescent pack. "His name is Fletcher. He's…um…how do I say it?" She searched valiantly for the proper PC term but came up short. "Special needs," she settled on. "He's been held back a couple years," she motioned to her own head, rotating her index finger around her temple in the universal hand gesture for "fucking nuts." "Sometimes we don't know where to put him. If he starts to get disruptive, we'll pull him."

*We'll pull him*? I thought. It sounded like code for "We'll take him out and *ice* him. Eighty-six him." Then I wondered if the poor son-of-a-bitch had any clue how many people looked on him as a pain in the ass.

I no sooner *thought* that than Fletcher yelled above the din, "Pain in the ass," and let out a cheeky chortle.

The principal shot Fletcher a look that would melt steel while I looked at him in stunned amazement. It was just plain odd. But maybe it was a *coincidence*. Yeah. Right. How many times had I used that old saw of an excuse to rationalize an occurrence that defied reasonable explanation?

The kids were told to quiet down, and the floor was turned over to me. Suddenly, I had thirty pairs of tiny eyes staring at me, waiting for wisdom to pour from my mouth. I'm not counting Fletcher in the pack, as he was staring into space at this point with his mouth loosely hanging open, like his jaw had broken hinges, and looking quite lost. It was a tough audience because they seemed at once curious and judgmental of me. I started talking with my usual cadence, which is crusty and forward. I don't have a "voice" for kids and a "voice" for adults. It's all the same voice, and I think my tone kind of scared some of the kids in the front row because I saw them leaning back in their little seats. That made me feel uncomfortable, so I attempted to change my voice to make myself sound "safer" but then I started to sound like I was tripping on Halcyon. I was reminded of Sergeant Weyler's admonishment before I left DH. "Watch your mouth, Jane," he warned me. I have a tendency to use crude language, which my job tends to perpetuate. Frustration was building by this point and I *thought*, "Fuck this shit." It wasn't a second later that Fletcher jerked his head away from the window and screamed, "Fuck this shit!"

Half the class giggled as the other half said, "Ooooh." The principal was about to "pull him" when I intervened. I told her to let Fletcher stay. The fact was I wanted to try a quick experiment. I *thought*, "Hey, Fletcher. Calm down. Can you hear me?"

I swear to God, the kid stared at me and said, "Yeah! I'm calm."

The rest of the classroom time is a blur. When I opened the floor to questions and answers, it went something like this:

"Can I touch your gun?"

"Is that a real gun?"

"Can I touch your gun?"

"You ever kill anybody with that gun?"

"Hey, seriously, can I touch your gun?"

"Did you ever shoot yourself by mistake with your gun?"

"Hey, lady cop, can I *please* touch your gun?"

Finally, the teacher piped up and introduced a new question. She wanted to know if there was any adage that I've learned from being a detective. I *thought*, "If you get a call that there's an incident on Colfax Avenue, it's a guarantee that someone's been capped." Not a half second later, Fletcher raised his right hand with his thumb and index finger positioned like a gun and softly said, "Bang!" But then, instead of staring out the window again, a look of sorrow filled his face and he buried his head on his desk.

I turned to the teacher and came up with the first clean, age-appropriate answer I could think of. "I learned that you can't judge a book by its cover," I offered. She seemed disappointed in the answer, so I elaborated. "In my line of work, criminals don't always look like what you all see on television.

Sometimes the bad guys look like the good guys. Sometimes the clean-cut person is really a monster and sometimes the strange-looking ones are the kindest." I tried not to look at Fletcher when I said that, but out of the corner of my eye, I could see him peeking out from where he'd buried his head in his arms. He was sizing me up.

"So how do you tell the good guys from the bad guys if you can't judge a book by its cover?" the teacher asked me.

"You listen to your gut and let it guide you."

I could see that she had no damn clue what I was talking about. We all have the ability to use our intuition, but we've been conditioned to always let logic override the process. Hey, I'm all for using logic; God knows I incorporate logic all the time, especially when I'm listening to a perp's interrogation and I hear an inconsistency in his/her statement. But you need to use a blend of logic and intuition. Too much logic and you ignore your gut; too much intuition and you lead with your heart more than your head. But it was obvious from the look on the teacher's face that she'd been programmed to call a spade a spade even though it might actually be a shovel.

Outside in the parking lot, I was walking to my Mustang to finally get the hell out of this pedagogic prison when I suddenly heard a voice behind me.

"Hey, cop lady!"

I spun around. It was Fletcher. Usually, people can't sneak up behind me. "Hey, kid," I said, trying to hide my startled self.

He leaned forward. I could see clearly how horribly his left eye was injured. The eyelid dropped over the outside of his eye while the eyeball itself was straining to the left. Three scars, varying between two and four inches in length, cut across his left cheek and temple. He gave me his goofy grin.

"I like the way you think, cop lady," he said, tapping his finger to his head.

I have to tell you that I felt like I was in a dream at that point. This couldn't be happening, but it was. "You read minds?" I asked him.

Fletcher stared into the sky and then to his right, suddenly lost in the moment. "I hear...and I see," he said. Then he looked me straight on. "*I see*. But they don't listen. But I can hear you and I can see you....You're real. Your cover *is* your book!"

It was his callback to my "You can't judge a book by its cover" comment. But then he started rambling and not making any sense. Poor kid. I hope the asshole who did this to him went down hard for it. "What happened to you, Fletcher?" I asked, motioning to his face.

He quickly covered his left eye with his left hand, as if to protect him from the memory. "Jack and Jill went up the hill and Humpty Dumpty had a great fall. All the king's horses and all the king's men couldn't put Jack together again."

"You fall?" I asked.

"Yeah. Pow! I fall down. Pow! I fall down. *Pow*! I fall down and don't get up. And then, nothing. All black," Fletcher explained, still sheltering his face. "But I'm lucky. At least I'm not in the wall."

"In the wall?" I said, furrowing my brow.

"Yeah. In the wall. Bull's-eye marks the spot."

I was about to disregard him but something...something pulled me in. "What are you talking about?"

"There was an old woman who lived in a shoe, she had so many children, she didn't know what to do, when the bough breaks, the cradle will fall and down will come baby, cradle and all. Bulls-eye marks the spot."

Fletcher looked at me with probing eyes. For a millisecond, he was normal. The soul inside him that hadn't been beaten to a pulp bled through his brown orbs and reached out to me in a desperate plea.

"Fletcher!" a voice yelled out.

I looked up and saw the principal making a beeline toward my car. Fletcher quickly backed away from me. The principal gave the kid a tongue lashing for being off school grounds and having the nerve to talk to me. She told him to go over to the curb, sit on the bench and wait for the "special bus." Then she turned to me with a roll of her eyes and told me how terribly sorry she was that I had been troubled by the kid. I asked her to tell me his story.

"He's a mess," she stated, tossing her hand in the air dismissively. "His father beat him when he was a baby and on up until he was six years old. It wasn't until his father put him in a coma that the state transferred him to foster care. He's bounced from one foster family to another. He's got special needs, since he has seizures due to the beatings. They said he suffers from something like a combination of autism and Tourette's syndrome. We're just warehousing him here until they can find a more suitable school." She leaned closer to me, talking to me as if I was her best buddy. "You want to know his biggest problem? He makes up stories that sound quite absurd. The social worker told me to ignore the fanciful tales. He's most likely rehashing some trauma from his childhood." She turned and saw Fletcher standing at the curb, staring into the sky. "Sit on the bench, Fletcher!" she screamed. Turning back to me, she shook her head. "Jesus Christ! Anyway, thank God he's with a decent foster family now. *The woman's a saint.* She takes in kids who have been abused and no one else wants. There's a place in heaven for her! I sure as hell could never do it!"

I asked her where Fletcher lived and she told me. "That's on my way back to DH. I can take him home." My first thought was that this *had* to be against school policy, but because I was a cop and wore a gun and ate up thirty minutes of classroom time that day, she figured I *must* be a safe bet. After all, don't most people believe that cops, ministers, teachers and doctors are all here to help us? If you judge a book by its cover, you sure do. She had no reservations about summoning Fletcher back over to my car and telling him to get in. Fortunately, I actually happen to be a trustworthy person.

The ride took less than ten minutes. Every time I tried to get him back on his odd tale about being "in the wall" and his disturbing nursery rhymes that suggested severe trauma, he just stared out the window. He was much more interested in making sounds like a car gearing up and down. I gotta tell you, I was regretting my decision to play the Good Samaritan, but I couldn't shake that damned feeling in my gut.

We rolled up to his foster family's home. It was in an extremely nice neighborhood. The two-story white house with green trim was beautiful, with a neatly mowed lawn, swept brick pathway and manicured hedges that framed the two front windows. Fletcher looked at the house and then stared out the front window of the Mustang.

"What is it?" I asked him.

He looked quite pensive and said nothing for a bit. "There was an old woman who lived in a shoe...she had *way* too many children and she didn't know what to do..." He turned to me and his eyes pierced me. "Time to go to sleep, baby. Bulls-eye marks the spot."

The front door of Fletcher's foster home opened. A large-framed woman wearing denim jeans and a white tunic trimmed in red walked out, holding a toddler in her arms. "Fletcher? Is that you?" she called.

Fletcher bowed his head and picked at my passenger seat. He made a strange grunting sound like a pig sourcing out food. The woman approached the car and I got out. Here was the "saint" I'd heard about from the principal. She had a cherubic face, blond hair cut to precision around her cheeks, and she wore a splash of soft blue eye shadow that accentuated her hazel eyes. A dainty gold cross adorned the outside of her white tunic and a simple gold wedding band graced her chubby ring finger. The toddler in her arms obviously suffered from Down syndrome.

"The school called and told me you'd be bringing Fletcher home," she said, smiling. "You're sweet to do that! Thank you!"

Nobody has ever called me "sweet." *Ever.*

"I'm Christy! We're just about to sit down to some milk and cookies! Want to join us?"

Nobody has ever invited me in for milk and cookies. *Ever.*

I looked inside the car and saw Fletcher rocking back and forth. While I wasn't certain, I'd heard that might be a sign of a child reliving trauma. I didn't want to leave the kid like that, so I accepted the cheerful broad's invitation. Besides, my curiosity was piqued. I wanted inside that house.

The mêlée that erupted there was jarring. A long table was set up in the large living room, and it was covered with a heavy plastic cloth that had been permanently stapled to the table. Ten children, ranging in age from around three to twelve years, sat at the table. Well, I say "sat," but I really mean hovered. Nobody was seated. Some were lying halfway on the table, some were under the table and one was on top of the table. Christy introduced me to her two

"angels" — teenage girls from her church who were in train-
ing to work with special-needs children. "They were sent
from heaven!" Christy gushed. The two pasty-faced girls,
who had only been with Christy for about a month, were
earning credits toward their college degrees by volunteering
and assisting with the children. Boy, that Christy really *was*
a saint. She wasn't just helping out the eleven special-needs
kids; she was also giving the gift of hands-on education to
these innocent high school girls. When I told her she must
have a busy schedule, she shook her head. "I'm just doing
our Lord's work," she said earnestly. "He spoke to me several
years ago and told me that I was to be his beacon of light
in the darkness of these poor children's lives. And when the
Lord speaks to me, I have no choice but to follow His word."

I wondered if the Lord also told her to wrap her table
in that hideous plastic cover, but I held back. The noise in
the place was starting to grate on my last good nerve. I could
feel the urge for a cigarette rearing up, so I knew I had to
make this visit a short one. Christy handed off the Down
syndrome child to one of the helpers and told the kids, including Fletcher, to take a seat at the table and be quiet. That
took another ten minutes because one of the toddlers blew
lunch on the carpet. Once they were all settled, they were
instructed to hold hands and Christy led a prayer over the
milk and cookies. She didn't realize it, but I was saying my
own prayer simultaneously. It went something like, "Dear
God, get me the fuck out of this hellhole." I no sooner said,
"Amen," than Fletcher let out a loud guffaw and looked up
at me, winking his good eye. That simple reaction reminded
me why I was there.

I asked Christy if I could use the restroom as a ruse
to check out the joint. Since the milk and cookies were free
flowing in the living room and the kids would soon be high as

a kite on sugar, I figured I'd have an easy roam of the large house without any interruption. But as I left the room, I stole a glance at Fletcher. He was trying to give me a not so subtle clue as he kept dipping his head to the floor and pointing that one good eye toward the kitchen.

*The kitchen?* I thought. He nodded, *really* pointing his head toward the floor as he did it.

*This is the first floor,* I thought. He shook his head at me.

*There's a basement?* I thought while realizing that this entire mental conversation with him "defied logic." Fletcher nodded.

"Let's sing Him our praises!" Christy exclaimed, as she led the motley collection of cookie-crunching characters into "What a Friend We Have in Jesus."

It was the perfect time to duck into the kitchen. Obviously, I didn't have a lot of time to "feel" the scene as I usually do. My eyes traced the large yellow kitchen with the happy-face clock and the collector plates on the wall, each with a verse from the New Testament scrolled on them. *Cheerful.* That's exactly how anyone would describe this kitchen. And *neat.* God, for a woman who had eleven special-needs kids, the kitchen was immaculate. The adage on the dish towel said it all: A clean home is a godly home. I've always thought that a clean home is a sign of a wasted life, but what the hell do I know?

A series of eight engraved plaques covered the length of the wall above the sink. It seemed that Christy had been honored by eight different organizations in Denver for her "tireless dedication" to special-needs children. I've been presented with three plaques in my life — two for saving people's lives — and I couldn't tell you where in the hell they are located if you held a gun to my head.

A large chalkboard filled the wall on the other side of the kitchen. On it was written: "What are we grateful for?" followed by ten answers that I was pretty sure Christy wrote in somewhat erratic handwriting. "Jesus" was the first answer, with "This Home" and "Christy" ranking numbers two and three, respectively. It was decent of Christy to give herself third billing after Jesus. It's important to stay humble.

I looked over to a door that held a calendar from her church along with eleven heart-shaped cutouts, each displaying a small photograph of a child in her care. I could understand why the school principal called her a *saint*. Christy was devoted, wasn't she?

*Wasn't she?*

Or was she obsessed? Or controlling? Or manic? Or fucking nuts? Or all of the above?

To the untrained eye, this kitchen was the epitome of a family- and God-centered home and the woman in the other room leading the group through the third verse of "What a Friend We Have in Jesus" was the quintessential queen of devout selflessness. But to me, it was organized chaos. Every item in that yellow room was a piece of a puzzle and the puzzle was starting to feel like madness incarnate.

My eye traveled back to the door with the eleven heart-shaped cutouts and photos. They were joined one by one with a white satin ribbon that was perfectly stapled to the door to form an elegant arrangement. Christy was a perfectionist. That much I could verify. But a glance back to her handwriting on the chalkboard told me she was easily excitable and prone to sudden, possibly violent reactions to stress. Yes, I have studied graphology, and it's come in damn handy at times. When you put a perfectionist who is prone to sudden, violent reactions in a situation where there is chaos every day, it can be like putting a match to gasoline.

I was suddenly reminded of Fletcher's nursery rhyme patter: "There was an old woman who lived in a shoe… she had *way* too many children and she didn't know what to do…" And then, "Time to go to sleep, baby. Bulls-eye marks the spot."

I looked closer at the white satin ribbon that joined the eleven heart-shaped cutouts with photos. On the third photo it was clear that the ribbon had been cut and retaped to the next photo. Could she have simply run out of ribbon? Maybe. But knowing how perfectionists operate, she would have been more likely to redo the entire display to avoid an interruption in the design. But if something changed in the design — if a photo had been removed, for example — it would easier to cut the ribbon like she did and join it to the next photo in the line.

I started to get a sick feeling right about then. It came on faster than food poisoning from bad tuna. I checked to make sure Christy was still occupied leading the afternoon songfest with her off-key pack of kids. And indeed she was. I opened the door that held the calendar and cutouts and was greeted by a set of steep stairs that led into a basement. The door creaked as I closed it and pulled the cord on the overhead light to illuminate my descent into the musty, dirt-floored habitat. As my feet hit the bottom, I was immediately struck by the dampness of the area. Moist conditions tend to accentuate other odors, such as feces and blood and death.

I turned on another light at the foot of the stairs. The walls were brick with cracked mortar.

And then I felt it.

I saw the desperation in the child's eyes.

I felt the fear spreading across the dank space.

I sensed the suffocating torture of dying slowly at the hands of a crazy woman.

Fletcher told me, "Bulls-eye marks the spot." I canvassed the small basement and saw a large dartboard hanging on the far wall, near the corner. The center of the dartboard had a red dot...a bulls-eye. I quickly crossed to the spot and removed the dartboard. Behind it, I found a section of bricks about eighteen inches tall and twelve inches wide that had obviously been removed and put back in place. Finding a crowbar nearby, I easily lifted the bricks away from the dirt. The smell of death gave it away long before my fingers touched the fingers of the baby.

It's taken me several weeks to process all this. I learned fairly quickly that Christy killed the baby before the two teenage girls went to work for her. I also found out that Social Services hadn't been making regular checks at her home because, after all, she was a multi-award-winning, thoughtful, cheerful, church-going, Christian woman who had been given the moniker of "saint." Nobody could have guessed that Christy was on high doses of four strong drugs to fight severe bipolar disorder and depression and that she'd stopped taking two of them, which pushed her into a cascading psychotic break. At the moment when her mind splintered, she was holding the baby who wouldn't stop screaming and that's when she probably said, "Time to go to sleep, baby," and proceeded to suffocate it before burying it half-alive in the wall of her basement. The problem was that Christy was so out of it, she didn't see Fletcher watching the whole thing as he hid in the basement behind the water heater.

I don't question how a woman can do that to a baby. I know that evil lingers in the minds of everyone. It just takes the right fuse to ignite it. I know that people looked at my own father and thought he was a great man. I also know that I didn't have a chance in hell of convincing anyone that he was a monster and that my brother and I were at his mercy. You can't judge a book by its cover.

And I don't question how a fourteen-year-old boy can emerge from the bowels of hell with only a small part of his brain functioning and be able to speak to me with his mind. I don't question the "coincidence" of being chosen that day to speak at Fletcher's school or the "synchronicity" that he "just happened" to be warehoused in the classroom I was in at that time.

And I *never* question my gut. Because my gut has gotten me where I am today. My gut allowed me to survive my own childhood hell and it's led me to solve homicide case after homicide case for more than seven years.

Writing about this whole ordeal has been cathartic for me. I feel a bit lighter right now. Maybe Sergeant Weyler was onto something when he suggested I do this. It sure as hell beats being psychoanalyzed by a Freud-loving woman with a mauve toilet.

# <u>YOU'RE ONLY AS SICK AS</u>

# <u>YOUR SECRETS</u>

My younger brother, Mike, is engaged to be married. Good for him. But the wedding won't be for an entire *year*. I personally don't understand long engagements. To me, it's either do it or don't do it, but don't keep me in suspense. I have to get him a present, and if he thinks it's not going to work with his fiancée, I'd like him to give me a heads-up so I don't have to keep track of the sales receipt in case I have to return his gift.

To further complicate my brother's whole engagement, he and his fiancée, Lisa, decided that they needed to drag it out by first having a "spiritual blessing" by a "shaman." Mike, if you're reading this (and I *know* you're reading this), why in the hell did we have to drag our asses across two states and end up in Sedona? If the attraction was the New Agers, we could have packed a lunch and driven over the hill to the Socialist Republic of Boulder, Colorado. It's infinitely closer than Sedona and I could have escaped the gathering sooner.

I hope Mike doesn't hire this "shaman" to marry him because I don't think that quack has a license to do anything except wave a turkey feather and blow sweetgrass smoke in your face. I keep putting "shaman" in quotes because when I think of a *real* shaman, I think of a four-foot, ten-inch, oily-skinned Peruvian male wearing nothing but a loincloth and a piercing stare and carrying a humble walking stick. I *don't* think of a bloated, sixty-year-old Jew who looks like Jack Klugman, wearing a Budweiser T-shirt and a *pressed* pair of dark denim jeans. Seriously. They were ironed. Who irons their jeans? Oh, that's right. Bloated, sixty-year-old Jewish "shamans" who drink Bud.

I know, I know. I come off as an abrasive cynic. But it comes with my job. I don't think anyone else at Mike's spiritual blessing gave this "shaman" a second thought. They just accepted him for whatever he said he was and left it at that. But not me. I looked at the "shaman" and pondered what thought process it took for him to craft this odd little image. I wondered what his distraught Jewish mother must think. "My son, the *SHA*man," I could hear her crying, with a roll of her eyes. Did he scour the Internet looking for "shaman props" to incorporate into his shtick? How many New Age workshops did he sit through in order to develop this ridiculous persona?

People are always saying I'm judgmental. Screw 'em. It's not judgmental; it's called *observation*. I suggest you learn it. If more people would take the time to observe other people and not just accept what they see on the surface as fact, they wouldn't have so many damn problems. I'm not saying they'd be happier; I'm saying their lives wouldn't be so complicated. As a cop, I can't help it. It's in my blood to probe beneath the surface. Once you learn the basics of reading body language, posturing, intonations and all the other subtle diagnostic tools good cops use to discern what's in front of them, you gotta go to the next level, and that next level is unexplainable. It's a *knowing* that grips you and leads you toward the truth.

With me, what you see is what you get. No illusions here. But I'm an odd bird in a flock of fakers. I looked around the crowd in Sedona as our "shaman" floated another cloud of sweetgrass across the air. God, what a motley bunch. Those who weren't standing in bare feet were wearing flip-flops. Who in the hell wears flip-flops to a damn "spiritual blessing"? I even spotted one guy wearing a tenement T-shirt. You know? Those sleeveless numbers that are ribbed and so thin you can see the outline of the guy's nipples if a cold wind blows? I thought this guy was waiting around to load up the folding chairs before we left for the "honoring of the elements" down by the water feature, but apparently he was a cousin of Lisa's. America, say hello to your future: It's wearing a damn tenement tee and flip-flops.

We're standing around this stagnant fountain that supposedly symbolizes "emotional freedom" as Mike and his future bride are repeating their "intentions" to each other and I can't take my eyes off this guy in the tenement tee. Lisa's cousin. I'm starting to wonder if maybe I busted him for doobie years ago. I've got a good memory for faces, and I can remember most of the boneheads I've taken down over the last two decades. But I can't figure this one out. Then he looks over at me and nods his head like he's acknowledging me. Now I'm really confused and I can't focus that much, especially after Mike and Lisa jump on their road bikes to cruise down the hill to the eco-friendly reception where *all* the food is green…even the cake. (I'm serious. I can't make up this shit.) I start to move toward the crowd and this wing-nut in the tenement tee makes a beeline for me.

"Hey, Jane," he says in a hushed voice, his orange flip-flops collecting another layer of dirt and gravel with each step.

He's looking more familiar at this point, but I still can't place him. I nod to him but keep up the wall around me.

"I guess we're gonna be related by marriage now," he says with a smile, "me the cousin of the bride, you the sister of the groom."

*God help me*, I'm thinking.

"This'll be a different kind of wedding for you and me, huh?" he says.

I bite. "Different in what way?"

"Well, for one, we'll remember it, and for another, we won't make asses of ourselves."

And *that* is when I knew where I've seen this guy. He sits across from me on the plaid couch with the bad springs in the basement of the Methodist church where they hold the weekly AA meeting.

For those of you who didn't get the memo, I'm sober. (I'm also back working in Denver Homicide after some "negotiations" with Sergeant Weyler. Now I'm *Sergeant* Detective Jane Perry, for what it's worth.)

I'm still getting used to regarding myself as a *recovering* alcoholic instead of a drunk. There's so much more to explain when you're *recovering* than when you're just another tedious, piss-ass alcoholic. People are more likely to accept you when you say you're a drinker, but when you're *recovering*, there are the inevitable questions of how long you've been sober, what prompted you to get sober, how does it *feel* to be sober, blah, blah, blah. If I made a habit out of indulging in all that shit, I'd have to get a load on just to suffer through it. I'm a very private person. I don't feel a need to wear my addiction on my sleeve and regurgitate my dramas to everyone in earshot. I prefer to stand outside the group and recover alone. But they say you need to have those fellow recovering drunk shoulders to lean on when you start, so I play the game...to a point. I don't have a sponsor. I just can't bring myself to get cozy with some well-meaning ex-alky who keeps insisting that I meet her for coffee so we can "chat." For me, it would feel like an Amway sales ambush. "Do you have a few minutes, Jane? I'd like to talk to you about your sobriety!" No thanks.

Am I keeping my sobriety a secret? Well, no, obviously not, since I'm writing about it and you're reading it. Did I keep my drinking a secret? Well, yes, in fact, I sure as hell tried. But I had a little trouble keeping the hangovers under wraps and my frequently bloodshot eyes tended to tip my drunken hat. But even so, there were still a few acquaintances who didn't quite appreciate how far I'd fallen into the bottle. But I'll say it again: *they weren't observant.* Just like Mike's Jewish "shaman," all I had to do was come up with a good cover story and more than one schmo bought this shiksa's lame excuses.

As they say in AA: "You're only as sick as your secrets." And let me tell you, there are a *lot* of people out there keeping a whole helluva lot of secrets. Our secrets often stalk us, continually reminding us that we're one revelation away from having our human frailties or youthful transgressions laid bare. Some of our secrets are minor, but other secrets

take on their own identity, framing and defining an individual's cloaked life. For those souls, their secrets haunt them,
holding them hostage to the fear that one day they will be
discovered. The mere thought of being exposed is enough
for a few of them to kill; for others, it's enough to make them
take their own lives rather than face disgrace.

As I've commented many times while working in
Homicide, people kill for one of three reasons: sex, money
or gettin' even. When you think about it, secrets inhabit each
of those motives: Sexual secrets, financial secrets and sundry
secrets that force a person to seek revenge. I had to keep all
of that in mind when I worked a case recently involving Mr.
Winston Gambrel.

I was paged at 2:22 a.m. a few weeks ago and sum-
moned to Mr. Gambrel's upscale home after Mr. Gambrel
hysterically called 9-1-1 to get help for his wife. She had
fallen down their circular staircase and sprawled in her lilac
nightgown on the Italian tile near their front door. When the
paramedics arrived, 65-year-old Gambrel answered the door
nude, hyperventilating and sweating profusely. His 59-year-
old wife, Abbey, showed signs of serious trauma on her chest
and shoulders. Tossed across the entryway, under an 18th-
century secretary from Britain, Abbey's lacy white underwear lay torn and slightly bloody around the lace edge. Mr.
Gambrel had surface cuts on his upper thighs. He told the
paramedics he didn't know how he got them but assumed it
was from scraping against the bedroom furniture as he sleep-
ily made his way through the darkness after he heard a loud
thump outside the upstairs bedroom door.

When his wife was pronounced dead, Mr. Gambrel went
into what I would best describe as catatonic shock. A deep
and soulful wail that cannot be manufactured by anyone

except those who honestly feel it in their bones followed that. "*She's my world*," he wept. As I stood there in the entryway, sealing the torn and bloodied lacy white underwear in a plastic Kapak evidence bag, I watched the world he knew crumble around him. Amid his grief, a gallery of suspicious eyes observed his every move. Among the paramedics and the other cops on the scene there was a sense that everything was not what it seemed. Mr. Gambrel's story of what happened also changed.

First he said he had awakened to a loud thump outside their bedroom, stumbled in the darkness toward the landing, turned on the light and saw his wife sprawled on the entryway tile floor. At that point, he claimed to have raced down the stairs and begun CPR, tearing off and discarding her underwear in the process because he thought he saw a puncture wound in her pelvis. The problem was that her lilac nightgown was not torn or bloodied, only her panties. There was also the question of the distance between where her body lay and the location of the panties under the secretary. When you fling lacy panties aside, they tend not to travel far, due to their weight. Also, a rough tile floor, such as the one in the Gambrels' entryway, prevents items such as lacy panties from scooting too far. Additionally, when I recovered said panties, they were pretty well hidden under the piece of furniture. It was that observation that generated a change in Mr. Gambrel's telling of the story.

With head bowed and eyes never locking with mine, Mr. Gambrel said that the lights in the house were already turned on when he awakened to find his wife missing from their bed. While he still maintained that he cut his nude body en route to the landing because of being half asleep, he claimed that when he descended the stairs, he had no recollection of removing her panties and tossing them aside. All he recalled was doing CPR and frantically trying to revive her. When I pressed him, asking why her panties were bloodied and seemingly hidden under the secretary, he maintained that he had no memory of removing them.

*No memory.* That's never a good answer, especially after you've already stated something else. But I'm patently aware of shock and how it can wreak havoc with recall. Shock can also create gaps in stories big enough for trains to chug through. Furthermore, interviewing a shock victim — especially someone who has just witnessed a loved one's death — can be problematic, since the shock tends to suspend one's reality, often making a person feel as if he is viewing the event from outside his body. The story is told from a more generalized point of view, rather than rife with detail, simply because shock creates a cloudy wash over the trauma. The mind says that "this can't be happening" and, thus, detachment begins to shield an individual from further emotional damage. It's the body's way of protecting itself, but it creates huge problems for a detective who is trying to piece together the puzzle.

One of the local cops on the scene made a comment out of Gambrel's hearing about what a "fine, upstanding guy" Gambrel was and how it was "too damn bad" that this event would fuck up that reputation. It was then that I realized who in the hell Winston Gambrel was. He and his wife owned and operated Abbey's Road Pub, a Denver downtown landmark. The name of the place was a play on words, combining the title of the Beatles' *Abbey Road* album with the name of Gambrel's wife, Abbey. The couple had no children and so their business became their "baby." Abbey's Road Pub celebrated all things British, from the ceiling that sported a

painted wall-to-wall Union Jack to the bevy of commemora-
tive plates that adorned each booth, with the Queen, Prince
Charles, the Queen Mother and Princess Diana featured.
But what I remembered most about his pub was the incredi-
ble collection of Beatles memorabilia that Winston Gambrel
had assembled over the years. You knew it had to be worth
something because he had all of it in cases, protected behind
heavy glass.

The Gambrels, both British, came to the States in early
1970 and opened their popular pub initially for tourists and
British transplants so they'd have a home away from home…
or pub away from pub. But the establishment quickly found
American fans who loved the Beatles' motif, imported ales
and lively atmosphere. In recent decades, Abbey's Road Pub
was the epicenter of all things charitable — from Run for the
Cure events to feeding the homeless on Thanksgiving Day.
They sponsored scholarships for adult literacy programs and
were well known for their annual Halloween festivities, where
they awarded a one-hundred-dollar cash prize to each of the
four people whose costumes and appearance best matched
George, Paul, Ringo and John.

While Winston Gambrel looked nothing like John
Lennon — his muscular and manly six-foot, four-inch frame
would have dwarfed the thinner and slighter Lennon —
Gambrel traditionally wore his John Lennon garb, circa
1969, to each year's Halloween party. His wife, Abbey, of
course, dressed like Yoko Ono. Photos of the pair in their
costumes were a regular feature every November 1 in the
"People" section of *The Denver Post*. As I walked up the staircase that led to the master bedroom, I studied the vast ar-
ray of photographs that lined the wall. The shots chronicled
Winston and Abbey's cherished moments at their pub over

the last forty years. Amid the crush of photos were forty shots — one for each year of the pub's operation — of their popular Beatles-themed Halloween parties. In the first shots, taken in the early 1970s, Winston obviously really had long, straggly hair that looked identical to Lennon's unkempt mane, along with the beard and mustache to complete the Lennon-like vibe. But as the 1970s melted into the 1980s and then the 1990s, it looked as if Winston cut his locks and switched to a John Lennon wig and paste-on facial hair. As each year passed, I noted, Winston's frame got a little heavier but his John Lennon costume never changed. From the cream-colored bell-bottom pants to the matching cream jacket and shoes, Winston Gambrel perfectly re-created the outfit Lennon wore on the *Abbey Road* album cover.

I checked downstairs and saw that Mr. Gambrel was seated on a chair, head in hands, as the paramedics zipped his wife's body into a black plastic bag and summarily lifted her onto a wheeled cart. There was no dignity to the whole thing, I thought. Here was the grieving husband and there was his wife, cold and dead, being zipped up like leftovers into a plastic baggie. Everything they shared before that moment was brutally truncated by fate and punctuated by the irreverent rip of a metal zipper. Every dream they dreamed ended at that moment; every knowing glance they shared across the breakfast table would be at the mercy of Mr. Gambrel's heartbroken memory. *Shattered.* That's the best way I can describe that man at that moment. *Gutted.* That's what he looked like as he reached out and achingly touched the plastic bag one last time as they carted Abbey's body out the door.

I knew what the cops were thinking downstairs. *Nice acting job, asshole.* We're all skeptics at any death scene. We

always see the worst in everyone because we've seen the shit-
hooks of humanity and what they are capable of doing to
their loved ones. To most of us, you're not innocent until
proven guilty; you're a suspect until we can find the real per-
petrator. And when I find a pair of your wife's panties with
bloodstains hidden under a piece of furniture…well, what
can I say? It's not leaning in your favor.

I continued up the stairs to the master bedroom. The
light on the landing was on. That was what Mr. Gambrel told
me in his first telling of the story. I flicked on another switch,
which partially lit up the master bedroom. Walking into the
bedroom, I turned on another light and gazed around the
dark wood-paneled room. My first thought was that it reminded me of the kind of elegance you might find in an
English castle. There was the king-size four-poster that sat
so high up, one would need a small step stool to comfortably
get in. A stone fireplace across from the bed had a wrought
iron emblem that looked like a royal crown and the words
"Hail Britannia" beneath it. I've always wanted a fireplace
in my bedroom because there's something quite calming to
me about going to sleep with only the amber light from a fire
and the reassuring crackle of the logs spitting embers onto
the stone. It's like camping, minus all the annoying shit. I
stood there for a second and imagined Winston and Abbey
curled up in their high-rise bed staring at the roaring fire and
talking about their long day at the pub.

Walking around to the foot of the bed, I turned on a
decorative lamp that stood on a small table. I determined
that Winston slept on the right side of the bed based on the
fact that on the left side table, there was a jar of jasmine-
scented hand cream, a box of pink Kleenex, and a small
photo of Winston. Call it preschool deduction, but that had

to be Abbey's side of the bed. I stepped back and retraced the most likely steps that Winston would have taken in the dark if, as he claimed, he had made his way around the bed and out the door. There were those surface cuts on his upper thigh, some of which had bled, that had attracted the attention of the cops on the scene. From what I could see, his alleged route showed several telltale signs of recent travel. For example, a framed photo was on the floor beside the small table that held the decorative lamp. A pair of slippers were several feet apart, as if someone had stumbled over them. Signs of a physical altercation in the room? Maybe. I peered closer at the corners of the bed but the dark wood made it difficult to see major blood transfer. Mr. Gambrel initially said that he tore off his wife's lacy panties because he thought he saw a puncture wound in her pelvis. But there was no puncture wound anywhere on her body.

I went back to those motives for murder: sex, money and gettin' even. That's where the secrets like to play. When you have bloodied lacy panties, you've gotta consider rough sex gone wrong or rape. It didn't mean that he killed her on purpose. Working out this twisted scenario in my head, I wandered onto the landing off the bedroom and tried to picture the possible ways this could have gone down. Abbey and Winston could have been going at it on the landing; maybe he rubbed against something sharp and transferred his blood onto her panties. Perhaps that's when he ripped them off her body and tossed them downstairs, which would make more sense given their final location. But without getting too graphic here, no matter how many sexual positions I tried to visualize the Gambrels engaged in, I couldn't find any sign of activity on the landing nor could I figure out how they might have been having sex in order for Abbey to land in the manner she did. Even though Winston said he turned her over to do CPR, the manner in which she was initially sprawled — again, according to Winston — indicated that she fell forward down the stairs. Of course, Winston could have lied to us about how he found her body, but my initial take was that his telling of that part of the story truly seemed genuine. What I didn't buy was his second version of the story, when he had his head lowered and never looked me in the eye. That was guilt showing through. What that guilt was connected to, I didn't know yet.

One of the first cops on the scene called up to me at that point. Mr. Gambrel was now in the other room. "There was no sign of sexual penetration on the deceased," he offered, as if he somehow knew I was up there visualizing the Gambrels getting frisky.

Okay, I thought, cross sex off the list. That left money and gettin' even. But this was spouse-on-spouse, which revolved in its own orbit. And that orbit is known as *rage*. Typically, you kill your spouse because you find out he or she is cheating on you. It can be premeditated but it's usually a boiling hot explosion wrapped in a blinding primal frenzy that starts with a verbal confrontation, graduates to throwing and breaking various household items, and escalates to a full-blown physical fight that leads to the death that lawyers justify as a "crime of passion." I thought about how shattered Mr. Gambrel looked. If that was an acting job, the guy should get an agent and go to Hollywood. As far as I was concerned, he loved his wife with a depth most people never experience. But that kind of unflagging devotion could certainly make the pain of finding out she had a lover even more cutting, which *could* result in a swift and sudden fight to the death. And yet, where was the proof of this violent fight?

Aside from that knocked-over photo and scattered slippers, I was coming up short.

I returned to the bedroom and righted the photo that had fallen off the small table. I couldn't help but smile. It was an obviously old shot of our man Winston Gambrel personally re-creating the cover of the *Abbey Road* LP in his cream John Lennon suit. There he was, all alone, walking across the real Abbey Road in London, caught in long stride. But he didn't look like he had on a wig or fake beard and mustache in the photo. I opened the back of the frame and pulled out the photo, turning it over. Printed were the words: Me on abbey road, December 1, 1969." Ah, he was a Beatles fan even back then.

I meandered around the bedroom, opening up drawers and closets. I memorized the contents of the drawer in Abbey's side table. I discovered a media closet that housed at least several hundred CDs. Of course, he owned every single Beatles album, but he also had every solo effort that John Lennon recorded. Oddly, there was nothing in there of George, Paul or Ringo's solo projects. In the corner of the closet, I found a small, unmarked box of reel-to-reel tapes. They were all dated 1969. As I shuffled through them, I only found one that was labeled: "proper elocution." I thought back to when Winston was wailing after hearing that his wife was dead. "*She was my world!*" I heard him say. I had detected something off at that moment in the entryway but I had nothing to link it to, so I just stuck it in the back pocket of my memory. But now I replayed those words as I had heard them downstairs. Oh, those buried secrets. They do tend to rise up at the most inopportune times. Buried reel-to-reel tapes on proper elocution from the late 1960s. What else was buried?

I strolled over to the walk-in closet. It was immaculate and was big enough to hold a compact car. The left side held all of Abbey's clothes and shoes, while the right side belonged to Winston. I closed the door, turned on the light and soaked it in. It wasn't the smell of the cedarwood or the beautifully crafted shelving I cared about. I was marinating in the vibe, letting my mind's eye root out the surreptitious clues. I took a few steps forward, touching the smooth handles of the wooden drawers that lined Winston's side of the closet. I was drawn inexplicably to a small brown, unmarked box pushed to the back of the top shelf. There was no way to reach it without getting on a stepladder. Thus, it was either something Winston didn't need often or something he wanted to make sure was out of the way. I went into the bedroom, grabbing a chair and the fireplace poker. Back in the closet, I stood on the chair and used the curved tip of the poker to drag the small box toward me.

It was sealed shut with heavy tape. I cut through the tape with the side of my car key and opened the box. There were only three items inside. Three items that someone in that house was hoping would stay buried forever. I collected them, sealed up the box, and replaced it on the shelf so that Winston would never know I had been there.

But somehow, I knew I wasn't finished in there. I stood back and stared at the columns of shelves and drawers that lined Winston's side of the closet. Something tugged at me. This happens to me a lot on the job. It's like a pull on my sleeve that holds me back and forces me to stay focused. When I get in that moment, it's like I fall into the void. All sound disappears and a guiding force takes over. It's the hand of God or justice, depending upon the innocence or guilt of the individual involved. My eyes canvassed the area. And that's when I saw it sticking out from one of the drawers nearest the door. I opened the drawer and pulled out the items, one after the other. I examined the tags and then replaced each one exactly the way I found it. I wasn't sure how this whole thing was going to play out, but I sure as hell hoped for a favorable outcome.

Four days passed. I got a call from the doc who had completed the autopsy on Abbey Gambrel. The cause of death was 100 percent certain. I got off the phone and took a deep breath and then rushed downstairs into the evidence room and signed off on the lacy panties I'd sealed in the plastic Kapak baggie. I was just getting off the elevator to walk back into Homicide when I saw Winston Gambrel standing in the hallway. I quickly secured the Kapak baggie behind my back. Gambrel looked disheveled, as though he hadn't slept in days. Under his arm, he carried a section of the Denver newspaper. He turned to me. Agony mapped his weary face.

"Detective," he said, his voice shaking. "I need to talk to you." The broad British *a* was pronounced when he said the word *talk*.

"I was actually just about to give you a call," I told him, watching him closely.

He didn't seem to hear me. Instead, he studied the carpet in a lost gaze. "My world is crashing down around me." Emotion overtook him and he began to weep. "Have you read today's paper?"

I shook my head, and he reluctantly withdrew the section he had tucked under his arm. The article, on the front page of the local section, featured a sensationalized story about the Gambrel case. From the little I scanned, the journalist who penned it intimated that "sources" suggested a sexual slant to the death of Winston's wife. While any mention of the bloodied lace panties was kept out of the story, the writer got around that by citing, "some investigators on the scene are considering whether a sexual motive led to the death of Abbey Gambrel." *Fuck*, I thought. I was the only investigator on the scene, so this "journalist" obviously got the story from some rookie cop who hadn't learned to keep his goddamn trap shut.

"I'm assuming that police searched my house that night?" Gambrel asked me, his eyes pooled with fear.

"I was the only one collecting evidence that evening, sir."

He looked at me, nearly paralyzed, for a hard minute. "I see."

"I was up on the landing. And in your bedroom."

The color drained out of Gambrel's face. He turned away, wiping his tears. "This could go to trial —"

"Sir," I tried to interrupt him.

"I can't go through a trial, Detective. This is killing me already. God, it's all so random."

*So random.* Yes. *It* is, I thought. "Mr. Gambrel, please —"

"I have something to confess, Detective," he said, looking me in the eye. "I killed...my wife...." He reached out and rested his arm on my shoulder as he dropped his head and sobbed.

I looked at Mr. Gambrel and watched the unrelenting pain course through his muscles. Waves of anguish rose and fell across his chest as he gritted his teeth and gripped my shoulder tightly.

I led him to one of our interrogation rooms and directed him to sit in one of DH's metal chairs, which leave a lot to be desired in the comfort department. I excused myself briefly, returning to my nearby office to retrieve several key pieces of evidence and information I would need for the conversation. I secured them, along with the Kapak, in a large manila folder. I also grabbed a tape recorder and a bottle of water from the refrigerator. When I returned to the tiny interrogation room, I found Mr. Gambrel with his head buried in his arms on the metal table. His brawny six-foot, four-inch frame barely fit beneath the table. "Here you go," I said, handing him the water.

He seemed dismayed by my gesture. "Do you always give cold bottled water to people like me?"

I thought about it and nodded. "Yeah. Actually, I do always give cold bottled water to people exactly like you."

"You're very kind," he said, dropping his head. "Too kind."

I knocked two quick raps on the two-way glass.

"What was that for?" he asked with a concerned look.

"I'm letting them know on the other side to start the video." I pointed up to the two corners of the tiny room where the video cameras were perched and pointed toward the table.

"You're filming this?"

"Yes, sir. Have to get it on record." I sat down and started the tape recorder. "That's my backup in case something goes screwy with the video."

Gambrel seemed overwhelmed. "How many people are behind the glass?"

"Two, I think," I said, opening the manila folder on my lap. Gambrel gazed at the two-way glass with great concern. "You thought this was going to be private?" I asked him. "Get used to it, sir. Confessing to murder can become a very public affair. Especially when it's someone as prominent and well-loved in the community as you."

"My world is crashing down around me." He tossed the Denver newspaper to the side.

That was the second time he'd said that in the last ten minutes. "Yeah, after we're done here, I'm going to call that news writer and show him some love. My job is tough enough without having a case tried in the court of public opinion. It can't help but infect a jury pool —"

"But I'm *confessing*," he said quickly. "That means no trial, right?"

"Your lawyer is going to fight you on that. They hate it when you confess."

"I don't want a trial," he stressed. *"That's why I'm confessing."*

"You know that you've got the right to remain silent? Anything you say can and will be used against you in a court of law —"

"Yes. Fine. Understood."

"No. I really have to finish this spiel. This is how the defense likes to catch us up later in court and I'm not going there." I rattled off the rest of his Miranda rights. "Take a sip of water," I suggested.

He took a rushed sip and shook his head. "You must think I'm awful."

I studied him. "You're not the first husband to confess killing his wife. You won't be the last." He looked at me briefly, pain laced in his blue orbs. "I see the guilt all over your face."

"You do?" He seemed shocked by my statement.

"Oh, yeah. I saw the guilt when I talked to you in the entryway of your house too. Guilt has a way of shadowing all of us. The things we strive to conceal from others tend to hide in the baggage around the eyes."

He was taken aback. "Really?" he said quietly.

"It's not obvious to everyone," I assured him. "You have to be *observant*. You have to know the codes."

"What codes?"

"If I told you that, I'd give away all my secrets and then I'd be an open book, and we can't have that now, can we?"

"I suppose not."

"You want a cigarette?"

"Excuse me?"

"A cigarette? Sometimes it helps to calm you down. I'm sorry I don't have any Dunhill ciggies to offer you —"

"Dunhill?" Gambrel looked at me, his mouth slightly agape. He gulped another sip of water.

"That's a fancy English brand? Lots of well-heeled Brits and celebrities favored them back in the day."

He was flustered. "Yes. I know."

"I figured you probably smoked those at some time in your life?"

"Is that right?"

"Well? Didn't you?"

"Yes." He paused. "But I quit."

"Well, good for you, Mr. Gambrel. I still can't give up the habit."

"Please call me Winston."

"Okay, Winston. You can call me Jane."

He furrowed his brow. "Friendly, aren't you?"

"Normally, no. Okay, so first question: where'd you go to college?"

He looked at me as if he didn't understand the question. "Excuse me?"

"College?"

"I thought…" He peered toward the two-way mirror and the video camera in the corner of the ceiling. "I thought I was making a statement —"

"Yes. We'll get to that. Right now I'd like to know where you went to college."

"Oxford," he stated without hesitation.

"Oxford."

"Yes."

"What years did you attend?"

He rubbed his forehead. "I went from 1964 until mid-1969."

"The five-year plan is alive and well in England as well, eh? That's kind of a staid college for a guy like you. Didn't a lot of uptight prime ministers graduate from Oxford?"

"I…I'm not sure…"

"Really? I thought that was common knowledge —"

"Yes, of course, you're right. Quite right."

"Just because I'm an ugly American doesn't mean I don't know a little bit about the motherland. Getting back to Oxford — I know it screams British just like tea and crumpets, but you seem like a fellow who would prefer a more outside-the-box, liberal education. I mean, your pub is not exactly a religious experience unless you worship the Queen Mum."

He appeared baffled by my banter. "When can I begin my statement, Jane?"

"In a second. I need to cover some basics for them." I gestured behind me toward the two-way glass. "Would you agree that you're a guy who is more of a free spirit?"

He looked flummoxed but he answered. "Yes. I would say that was true."

"Always have been?"

"Yes. I don't understand where this is —"

"Is that what drew you and Abbey together?"

He was silent as a sad smile crept across his face. "Yes."

"Was she an English rose or a wild child of the '60s?"

"I would have to say the latter. England couldn't contain her. She dreamed of hopping across the pond to America to find the freedom she longed for."

"And you? Did you want to experience America's freedom?"

His eyes strayed from mine. "Of course. Land of opportunity. I always wanted to experience it. I'd never been here."

I looked at him pensively. "When did you and Abbey meet?"

"Late October of 1969."

"Did she take that photo of you crossing Abbey Road?"

Winston looked slightly aghast. "Yes. She did. How did you —"

"It was toppled over in your bedroom. You looked like a young John Lennon in that photo."

"Thank you."

I looked at him. "Why'd you say thank you?"

"I —" He struggled. "I don't know."

"Obviously that observation doesn't insult you, right?"

"Why would it insult me?"

"Of course it doesn't. You dress like John Lennon every year for the Halloween party at the pub. And you wear the same outfit at those parties that you wore in the Abbey Road photo." I could see he was getting uncomfortable. "You liked John Lennon, didn't you?"

"Yes," he said carefully.

"You connected to him in some way. His tough childhood?" I looked at Gambrel's eyes but he wasn't relating to that comment. "His free-thinking ideology?" He arched his eyebrow. *Bingo*. We had a winner. "Well, of course. That was Lennon's draw for you. He represented an off-the-wall, British outlook you respected."

"Quite right," he said nervously.

"Yeah. Quite right. Where were you born, Winston?"

His eyes skirted again to the two-way mirror. "Is this the typical sort of questioning that is done when one is confessing to murder?"

"I don't know if there's any 'typical' questioning. This isn't like, what's that British cop show on PBS? *Prime Suspect?* It's not like that. So, where were you born, Winston?"

"Cheltenham."

"Prosperous area. Not far from Oxford."

"Right."

"That's convenient. A short hop to the ol' alma mater. You grew up with some means?"

He looked me straight in the eye for the first time. "Yes. I did."

"Which helped you open Abbey's Road Pub."

"Very much so." He looked down at the table, a wave of sadness washing over him as a memory appeared to crop up unexpectedly.

"Are you okay?"

He swallowed hard and let out a hard breath. "Yes. I'm fine. Just quite tired."

"Yeah, fatigue tends to do strange things to a person. Defenses are lowered. You're not as sharp as you should be." Winston looked at me warily. "For example, you should have an upper-crust British accent. And yet, you don't. That's the thing about the Brits. They still have levels of status that structure their existence. And each level of status has a unique enunciation." I tapped my ear. "But you gotta have the ear for it." I leaned back in the chair. "My sergeant — Sergeant Weyler — he only watches PBS. I think he figured I needed some class in my life, so he taped a bunch of episodes of shows he liked. *Prime Suspect* was one. But the series that struck me the most was a classic called *Upstairs/Downstairs.* I'm sure you know it. It's the upper class who live upstairs versus the working class who live downstairs. *Upstairs/ Downstairs.* Clever, eh?" I could see Winston squirming. "I watched a bunch of episodes and it was pretty damn good. And I started to get tuned into what a working-class accent sounded like versus that upper-crust intonation the wealthy class adopt. There's quite a difference. And the two of those accents *never* meet. You either speak the working-class or the tight-ass wealthy dialect. And if your status changes from poverty to wealth, your accent does not. Look at John Lennon. He grew up in a rough working-class area, and after he acquired all the money and fame, he never adopted an upper-crust pronunciation. The opposite is also true." I leaned forward. "You don't grow up with means, as you told me you did, and sound like you're from Liverpool. Your generation doesn't slum like that."

Winston cleared his throat and sat up straighter. "Spend as much time in America as I have and your accent gets lazier. Ask any transplanted Brit. People even say I sound American at times."

"Do they? Is that when you get tired at the end of a long day? Or talk in your sleep?" I leaned forward. "Or become emotional? Is that when your American accent creeps through?"

His chin began to tremble. I caught his eyes checking out one of the cameras in the corner of the room.

"When you were informed of your wife's death," I continued, "I heard you say, '*She's my world*.' And you said it with an American accent. It was one of the realer moments of your life because your defenses were down. That's when the truth creeps out of a person. Shock takes over and you step outside yourself. But that wasn't the first time shock overwhelmed you, was it?"

Winston gripped the side of the metal table with his large hand. "Please...can we not do this?"

I opened the manila folder and brought out the three items I'd borrowed from the small brown box I found on Winston's closet shelf. I laid the first one on the table as his eyes grew larger. "Recognize that? Those are ticket stubs to a Philadelphia Phillies baseball game. And the date clearly shows 1964. How about that? And then this." I revealed a beat-up royal blue basketball jersey with a faded number thirteen across the front. "Even though this was before my time, it only took me a few seconds on the Internet to identify this as a genuine Philadelphia 76ers fan shirt with Wilt Chamberlain's number. And what's more, Wilt autographed it!" I pointed to the faded signature on the back of the jersey. It looked like Winston's mouth went dry. I peered closer at the signature. "It's hard to make out Wilt's name. But it sure isn't difficult to make out the name of the guy he was signing it to. *Rick.*" I spread out the jersey in front of Mr. Gambrel. "Now, if this was bought on eBay, you'd have it hanging in one of those tempered-glass cases. You know? Like the ones you have all that Beatles memorabilia in at your pub. You'd want to show off this puppy. But instead, I found it stuffed in an unmarked box in your closet...with the tickets to that Phillies game in 1964. Now, you tell me how you were going to a Phillies game and having Wilt sign your shirt during the *same* time period when you were allegedly studying at Oxford in merry ol' England?"

He started to say something.

"Remember," I cautioned him, "anything you say can and *will* be used against you in a court of law, Mr. Gambrel. You told me you'd never been to America before you and Abbey flew over the pond and settled in Denver. So I advise you to not tell me that you made two separate trips in '64 and again sometime between '65 and '68 when Wilt was tearing it up for the 76ers." Gambrel sank back into his chair. "Then there's this." I slid a faded color photograph of a young Gambrel with his parents toward him. His eyes welled up. The shot showed the happy trio standing in front of the Liberty Bell in Philadelphia. The young Gambrel was clean-shaven and had short hair. On the back of the photo, it said: "Last photo of us. May, 1969." "You were twenty-three in that photo. One month away from graduating from college. Which meant you were one month away from the first time your world crashed around you."

Gambrel turned away, tears welling in his eyes. He seemed to be trying to shield himself from one of the cameras. "Please don't do this. I beg you."

"Bear with me, Rick," I said gently, "I have to do this." I brought out a single sheet of paper with an article I'd copied. "I did a simple search using the name Rick Gambrel in the archives of *The Philadelphia Inquirer* between May and December of 1969. It didn't take me long to locate this article about the car wreck you and your parents were in while en route to a family college graduation party." Gambrel stared at the article I slid in front of him. "They died instantly, and you, their only child, miraculously had only minor injuries. But it took the paramedics over an hour to free you from the wreckage." Tears fell freely from Gambrel's eyes. I looked at him with compassion, fully feeling the brunt of grief that choked his throat. "That was the longest hour of your life, I imagine. And shock took its predictable course."

Gambrel slid the faded color photo of his parents and him toward him. "One second we were talking about how I was going to spend the summer," he said, his British accent gone, "and the next, I was hanging upside down with my father's face shoved against mine. I felt his blood falling on my cheek and his skin slowly grow colder. I wanted to reach out to him but I was pinned. I kept telling myself it was a dream and that I was going to wake up." He looked at me. "And that's the way my life kept going for me. Like I was living in a dream. There were days when I hovered above myself. Reality was debatable. Large gaps of time were unaccounted for. I dissociated every day." As he relived that time of his life, it was clear to me that Gambrel obviously suffered from post-traumatic stress disorder — unfortunately, something I'm intimately familiar with. One's mere existence becomes questionable, at best. He continued. "The only thing that kept me somewhat grounded was music. The Beatles, most of all. I let my appearance go that whole summer of '69. People started saying, jokingly, that I looked like John Lennon with my beard and long hair. And that was okay because — you were right — I *did* identify with him in many ways. I wanted to be free, like I thought he was. I had to get away from Philadelphia and the memories. I sold the family house and everything in it. The only thing I kept was that 76ers jersey, the Phillies ticket stubs, and that photo. I have no idea why. I just needed something tangible that would remind me occasionally of who I used to be. But the truth was,

I couldn't stand being myself anymore because there was too much pain attached to that guy."

"And becoming British was pretty cool to you."

"Becoming John." He rolled his eyes.

"But calling yourself 'John' would have been too obvious, right? So, you opted for next best name. *Winston.* Lennon's middle name."

Gambrel shook his head. "You're good, Jane."

"You smoked Dunhill cigarettes because John Lennon smoked them." He nodded, shocked that I made that connection. "You bought some reel-to-reel tapes on proper elocution so you could speak with a proper British accent."

"God, you found them, too, eh?" He swallowed hard.

"Yeah, I opened up lots of closets and drawers."

Gambrel stared at me. I knew *exactly* what he was thinking.

"So, you went to England," I said, changing the subject.

"Yes, right," he said, trying to contain his anxiety. "But I still wasn't all there...up here...." He tapped his head. "But that all changed...when I found my Abbey." He smiled. "We met at a pub not far from Abbey Road where that photo was taken for the album. John Lennon was singing 'Give Peace a Chance' on the radio. She told me it was a kaleidoscope of synchronicities that meant we were destined to be together. Me, who looked like John Lennon, and her, named Abbey, in a pub on Abbey Road. And I believed her. She breathed light into my darkness for the first time since the accident. She fell in love with the image of who she thought I was. And I kept telling myself that it was okay to let her believe that, because deep down, my love for her *was* honest. When she told me she dreamed of going to America, I told her I'd follow her anywhere. I loved her sense of adventure and she…loved my eccentricities."

"Eccentricities."

He looked at the two-way mirror in a guarded fashion. "Yes," he said, barely above a whisper.

"When did you tell her about your past?"

He sheepishly looked at me. "Never." I couldn't believe it, but he was serious. "I wanted to, believe me. I kept thinking that I would early on in our relationship. But then, it became easier and more comfortable to be Winston Gambrel than Rick Gambrel. I liked Winston because my Abbey loved him so much."

*My God,* I thought. That's one helluva secret to keep under your vest. "And so you came to Colorado and lived happily ever after."

"Yes. *We did,*" he emphasized. "She was truly my soul mate."

I leaned forward. "But she was working fairly long hours, lately, wasn't she?"

"Yes. The pub is sponsoring two big events this month —"

"She wasn't getting a lot of sleep?"

Gambrel stared at me. "No. She had bouts of insomnia."

"So, she took something to help her sleep."

He eyed me carefully. "Sometimes…"

"A drug whose label clearly states that one of its side effects is sleepwalking." He looked at the two-way mirror and then back to me with pleading eyes. I leaned forward and whispered to him. "A secret is not worth keeping if it means you have to tell a greater lie." He bowed his head. "You asked me if I gave cold bottled water to people like you and I told you that I did. I don't, however, give cold bottled water to killers. And you are *not* a killer. When I met you by the elevator today, I was coming upstairs from the evidence room. Prior to that, I'd gotten a call from the coroner's office. The autopsy on Abbey showed that she died from the fall down the stairs and that she had ingested twice the recommended dose of the sleeping pill approximately two hours before she fell. Sleepwalking is my guess." Gambrel closed his eyes. "Furthermore, based on lividity, it appears that she lay there for at least an hour, dead, before you found her. The trauma on her body shows it was incurred post-mortem, when you were performing CPR."

Gambrel broke down in tears. "I felt such guilt that I didn't feel her get out of bed or hear her fall. The love of my life lay there dying on a cold tile floor while I'm asleep upstairs!" He pulled his fingers through his hair. "I just happened to stir and see she wasn't in bed and that's when I got up in the dark and bumped into the bed and the side table, cutting my hip. When I saw her lying in a heap at the foot of the stairs, I thought, Please, God! Don't take away another person I love so deeply in the blink of an eye! I pounded on her chest and I tried to breathe life into her, but it was no use."

"And that's when you called 9-1-1."

He wiped his tears off his face with his large hand. "Yes."

"But you felt guilt about something else, didn't you? Before the paramedics showed up, you removed these." Opening the manila folder, I lifted the plastic Kapak that held the bloody white panties and set them on the table in front of Gambrel. He stared at them in stony silence. "I was the only person on the scene who secured these in the Kapak. Nobody else bothered to check the tag. Size extra large. And your wife probably wore a small." Gambrel buried his head in his hand. "The paramedics came to the door. You remembered you had them on and so you tore them off and hid them under the furniture. The blood came from you when you cut yourself walking around the bed in the dark." I leaned closer to Gambrel. "You were willing to confess to *murdering your wife* to keep your secret fetish under wraps? My God, man. How does that become the *better* option?"

"Don't you see? You know how this tabloid world operates! Everything about my past would come out. My entire life would be up for ridicule. I would be the punch line on every late-night talk show. My image as the burly Brit who runs the landmark English pub and gives back to his community...all that would vanish. Nobody would care *why* my life turned out like this. They'd be too busy laughing and judging me. And all the good Abbey and I have done for forty years would be forgotten. I never told Abbey the truth about my roots but she did know about this." He glanced to the panties. "And she didn't care. John Lennon had his eccentricities and so do I. But the world will not be as kind as my dear wife was."

I glanced back at the two-way mirror and then turned back to Gambrel. "You see this writing on the Kapak? That shows who submitted the panties into evidence. That's my signature. And when I signed them out of evidence, I also left my signature. As you can see, nobody else signed them in or out. So I'm the only one who's really...intimately connected to them. And since your wife's death was ruled accidental," I broke the seal on the Kapak, "I have the authority to return your property to you." I handed him the panties. "You can throw them away or put them in the drawer on your side of the closet with the others."

He looked at me, genuinely thankful. Still, there was trepidation. "How can I trust *them*," he jutted his chin toward the two-way glass. "That journalist scored a story from some cop at the scene — a story that was pure conjecture. How can I be so sure that one of those people on the other side of the glass won't chitchat with a reporter?"

I turned to the two-way glass. "Because…there's nobody back there."

Gambrel was confused. "But —"

"And those cameras? If they were on, there'd be a red light indicating that. This interrogation room is actually out of commission while they remodel it."

Gambrel pointed to the tape recorder that was still on. "And that?"

"Oh, that's real. But it's just a prop. All secrets need sturdy props to make them more realistic." I turned off the tape recorder. "Look, when I saw you by the elevator, I was about to tell you what I'd learned from the coroner and give you back the panties. But then you confessed to murder and so I had to shift gears."

He tried to wrap his mind around everything. "So…just to be clear…you are the *only* one who knows any of this?"

"That's right. And once I call that reporter and tell him that your wife's death was an accident and then *strongly* urge him to write a glowing story about you and how much Abbey's Road Pub has done for the Denver community, there will not be a whisper of doubt or judgment about you from anyone." I stood up. "Go home, Mr. Gambrel. Grieve for your wife. And then go back to work when you're ready with your head held high."

"You don't judge me?"

"Because you pretend to be British?" I asked him. "Or because you changed your first name? Or because a big manly guy like you enjoys wearing women's panties? I'm a recovering drunk, Mr. Gambrel. I'll leave the judgment to the ignorant and to those who have never experienced their own dark night of the soul."

He left, and as I walked back to my desk, I remembered Gambrel's comment about how *random* it all was. He was talking about death — first his parents' death and then, forty years later, his beloved wife's. But there's a random quality to life too. Your parents die and you grow your hair long and start listening to The Beatles. Then you sell the family house, change your name, and travel to England, where you adopt an English accent and meet a girl named Abbey in a pub near Abbey Road while John Lennon sings "Give Peace a Chance" on the radio. The randomness of his parents' death was responsible for the randomness of finding the love of his life. It was actually a beautiful story, but, sadly, it was one that could never be revealed because it was born and ruled by the power of a secret.

And then I was reminded again of that Jewish "shaman" my brother hired for his spiritual blessing ceremony. I bet *he's* got one helluva backstory, too. I should introduce him to Mr. Gambrel. They'd have a lot not to talk about.

# THINGS AREN'T ALWAYS
# WHAT THEY SEEM

Detective Jane Perry walked down the snow-packed Denver sidewalk, the early morning air crisp and biting around her. She took a hard drag on her cigarette and then another, hoping it would settle her nerves, but that familiar knot in her gut remained. The snowy drifts and white landscape surrounded her, smothering most of the typical sounds one might hear on a city street, even at this hour. It was as though a pillow had been placed over Denver's streets, suffocating all but the screams.

She arrived at her destination, glancing down the street furtively. Mirrored stillness embraced her with an uneasy grasp. Above her head, the red neon sign of Bloody Mary's Bar glowed angrily against the traces of snow that had blown against the building. The bar was aptly named, Jane figured, given the brutal crime scene she'd left twenty minutes ago. Bathed in a grisly crimson slaughter, the smell of death was still ripe and stung Jane's nostrils.

It was just past 1:30 in the morning. She had less than thirty minutes before the bar closed. Jane hesitated briefly before inhaling a hard hit of nicotine and entering the establishment. Inside, she stamped the snow off her rough-out cowboy boots and shook her shoulder-length brown hair, letting the icy droplets fall against her leather jacket. Save for the jazzy background music, the bar was nearly as quiet as the street outside. A lone bartender stood behind the ornate western-style bar, wiping down the sink in an almost trancelike manner. The only other occupant, a blond-haired woman, sat at the far end of the bar, staring straight ahead and sipping a martini. She was dressed in an expensive white down jacket with black fur trim. A pair of designer jeans hugged her trim thighs and toned backside. Fur-trimmed white boots completed the ensemble.

The bartender looked up at Jane, his eyes hiding apprehension. Jane sat at the opposite end of the bar from the blond woman. She'd been told numerous times in AA that you don't willingly put yourself in situations or places that compromise your sobriety. But here she was. One-fucking-thirty in the morning. She eyed a bottle of Jack Daniels behind the bar, spotlighted beautifully and magnified in all its majesty against the large mirror that framed the rear of the bar. How many nights had she drained a bottle of Jack in the comfort of her own house, hoping that she could momentarily forget the carnage and float above herself in suspended animation? Jane shifted in her seat. The barstool felt strangely comfortable against her ass. Too comfortable. She could feel herself falling into that place where the voices entice; the ones that promise temporary solace with just one sip. Even though she had thirteen months under her belt and numerous sobriety chips tossed in her bedroom drawer, the triggers that prompted her to drink away the darkness were still present on a daily basis. And as tough as Jane appeared on the surface, the bloodbath she'd just seen could easily trip that trigger.

The bartender slowly made his way toward her. "I stop serving in ten minutes," he said, his eyes full of hesitation. "You want a drink?"

Jane smiled an uneasy grin. "Oh, yeah. I do."

The blond woman turned when she heard the sound of Jane's voice. "Jane?" There was a soft, familiar Texas drawl. "Is that you?"

Jane cocked her head to the woman, recognizing her. "Courtney," she said.

"Well…," Courtney said with a slight grimace, "this is embarrassing, isn't it?"

Jane addressed the bartender. "Hold that thought, would you?" She ambled down the bar toward Courtney. "Mind if I sit here?"

"Of course not. I could use the company."

Jane sat on the stool next to Courtney. Now that Jane was closer to her, she could see how much Courtney had aged. The last time they'd seen each other was about a year prior, at the annual Domestic Violence fundraiser that Courtney's husband sponsored. The vibrant blue eyes Jane saw then were now replaced by gray spheres that lacked any life force. This former Miss Texas beauty queen looked like she was in her mid-fifties rather than early forties, with lines carved around her mouth and into her forehead. Her deeply set eyelids — a creation of cosmetic surgery — appeared to be hollowed recesses that gave off an almost ghostly gaze. Her skin was pale and moist, as if she'd been sweating or was feverish. Gone were the false eyelashes Jane recalled her always wearing. Gone was the rocket-red lipstick that was so perfectly applied, it never smudged. The polished red finger-nails, Courtney's trademark, were still there. But this was the first time Jane had seen her manicure with gaping chips.

"Should I ask how you're doing?" Courtney gently said.

Jane cleared her throat. She was not one to open up to others, even when it might serve her. "I've had a shitty night. I'm pretty fucked-up right now."

Courtney reached out and touched Jane's hand. "I'm sorry."

Fresh images of the bloodbath flashed in front of Jane. She ran her fingers through her tangled hair, hoping in some way it would shift the deathly scene out of her mind. She looked at Courtney and felt a shudder down her spine.

"My God, Jane. I can feel what you're feeling right now. Is there anything I can do to help?"

Jane stared straight ahead. She had to focus. She want-ed to scream but she had to tamp down the anger and revolt that was rising up inside her throat. "No, really. It's okay, Courtney. Thank you, though."

The bartender spoke up. "Five more minutes before cut off."

Jane considered his words. She checked the large clock on the wall. It was nearly 1:40.

Courtney leaned closer to Jane. "Don't do it, Jane," she whispered. "It's not worth it. Believe me." Her eyes drifted to the half-finished martini. "I should know, right?" Courtney slammed the remaining alcohol and slid the glass forward. "One more, please," she instructed the bartender.

When had the desperation begun for Courtney? Jane wondered. When had the voices crowded into her head to the point that she could not ignore their demands anymore?

Jane remembered the first time she met Courtney in the basement of the Methodist church. She was shocked that a woman who was married to a public figure like Craig Gardner would have the courage to hang with the drunken riffraff and expose her vulnerabilities. She could call herself "Courtney M." all she wanted, but everyone in that room knew who she was. But they all played along and pretended that they'd never seen her face on the front page of *The Denver Post* when she and Craig were photographed with the governor-elect after his landslide win for the office. If you knew anything about anything, you knew that it was Craig Gardner and his outstanding public relations skills that made that astonishing victory a reality. You also had to forget that ten-page spread in *Architectural Digest* featuring the Gardners and their three blond children — a girl and two boys who ranged in age from four to twelve — posing like urban royalty in their Denver mansion and in their Telluride vacation home. Jane recalled the title of that pictorial: "Master of the (PR) House." It was framed over a shot of Craig leaning against his Bentley, arms crossed and staring intensely at the camera. Craig Gardner was a marketing alchemist, turning his clients' endeavors into gold and making himself a millionaire many times over. But all that had to be pushed aside when Jane sat across from Courtney M. at the weekly AA meeting.

And when Courtney M. told the group why she drank, it was obvious to Jane that everyone in that tiny basement room listened with more interest. It didn't matter that the woman who sat on the folding chair had a back story equally traumatic or that the guy squashed into the center of the couch with bad springs had gone to jail for nearly killing a child when he drove drunk. Courtney Gardner was a celebrity in the room, and when she spoke, people leaned closer to hear every tortured word.

But when Courtney saw Jane at the annual fundraiser or in public, she always made a point of approaching Jane and making a connection. It might have only been a few minutes of conversation, but it was meaningful and genuine each and every time. Maybe it was her lilting Texas drawl that took its time spilling from her lips, each word so clearly enunciated, it seemed to occupy its own zip code. Or perhaps it was the sincere way Courtney would hold Jane's hand or touch her shoulder in a compassionate manner. When Courtney would inevitably say, "If there's anything I can do for you, *please* let me know," Jane knew it came from her heart.

So, ironically, there she was seated at a bar with the woman, with Courtney asking Jane if there was anything she could do to help her.

The bartender delivered the martini and turned to Jane. "What would you like?" he asked with that same established reluctance laced through his voice.

Jane looked at him and swallowed hard. "You got a sparkling water and lime juice?"

The bartender glanced at Courtney and then back to Jane. "Yeah," he offered without moving.

"Well, okay." Jane waited but he still didn't move a muscle. "*I'll take it.*"

He shot another guarded glance at Courtney before walking to the other end of the bar to prepare Jane's order.

When he was out of earshot, Courtney leaned closer to Jane. "Good for you, Jane. You stayed strong. Don't mind him. He's been acting like that toward me all night since I came in here. He's a squirrelly fellow. I think he's been in trouble with the law." She took a dainty sip of her martini. "Does he look familiar to you? Criminally speaking, of course."

Jane glanced at the bartender. She caught a slight shake of his right hand as he poured the sparkling water into Jane's glass. "Never seen him before." She peered up at the flat-screen TV in the corner of the bar. An infomercial played, typical fare for nearly 2:00 a.m. It was programming that took full advantage of insomniacs' pattern of purchasing items they would never buy if they were fully alert.

"I asked him to change the channel when I arrived. He had the Channel 9 late news on." Courtney took another genteel sip of her drink. "Cynthia Naylor was reporting from the location of a grisly crime scene...." Jane looked at Courtney. "I noticed that the bartender got quite tense at that point, so I asked him to please change the channel." Another swig of the martini disappeared, this time less precise. "*Cynthia Naylor.* That muddle-mouthed, no-talent bimbo. Humph! *Naylor.* I just realized the irony of her last name. I do wonder how many men have *nailed* her?" She twisted her mouth into an unattractive smirk. "She thought she actually had the ability to steal Craig away from me. Poor little delusional bitch. Mark my words, Jane, she's destined for the glory dump of mid-market daytime-news anchoring."

Jane wasn't sure how to broach the subject, so she just dove in headfirst, tact be damned. "If you don't mind me asking, Courtney, when did you fall off the wagon?"

"Would you believe me if I told you it was tonight?" She took a healthy swig, as if to button her statement.

Jane studied Courtney's haggard face. "Really?"

Courtney picked at the red nail polish on her thumb. "Hand to God. It's not like I didn't think about it a *gajillion* times before now. And it's not like I didn't buy a bottle and bring it home only to pour it down the sink." She stared at the glass-topped bar, weaving figure eight swirls with her finger against the glass. "Life has been difficult, Jane." A thought crossed her mind, and she turned to Jane with a cheerful smile. "How is your little brother, Mike?"

Considering all the people Courtney knew, Jane found it astounding that she remembered her brother's name — a name she might have only mentioned once in passing at one of the AA meetings. "He's good. He's engaged to a girl named Lisa."

"Oh! How wonderful! I *do* love *love*! I'm such a softie for engagements and weddings! There's nothing more important than finding your soul mate and living your life as one heart."

The bartender brought Jane's water and lime and walked away. Jane took a much-needed sip. "You believe in soul mates, huh?"

"*Absolutely*!" Courtney swept the lemon peel seductively around the lip of the martini glass. "Are you seeing anyone?"

Jane sucked a long sip through the straw. This conversation was not what she'd planned. "No. It's all I can do right now to deal with my job and…you know…not fuck up my sobriety."

"Jane, look at me." Courtney leaned forward. Jane obliged. "Don't *ever* turn your back on love. Without love, the world's a terrible place to hang your hat."

Jane stared at Courtney. "Oh, Courtney…"

"What?" she asked quizzically.

"Courtney —"

"Wait a second." She strained to hear the song playing over the speakers. "Can you please turn that up?" she asked the bartender.

The bartender did as he was told. The warm, inviting opening strains of Etta James's "At Last" filled the bar.

Courtney smiled broadly and clasped her hands together. "Oh, Jane! This was our wedding song when we danced our first dance sixteen years ago! Isn't it *divine*?! 'My love has come along...my lonely days are over...'" Courtney softly sang along with Etta as she swayed on the barstool. "This song was my personal soundtrack for *so many* years."

"Is that right?" Jane said, ditching her straw and gulping the sparkling water.

Courtney looked at Jane's drink. "You need more lime in that, don't you?" She leaned forward and grabbed a piece of lime from a dish under the bar. As she reached for it, the white sleeve of her jacket pulled up, revealing a series of bruises — some fresh and others fading. Courtney plopped back in her seat and handed Jane the lime. "There you go, honey."

"Those are pretty bad bruises you got there," Jane said carefully, squeezing the lime into her water.

Courtney pulled down the sleeve of her jacket and stared at her martini.

"You okay, Courtney?"

She forced a well-worn yet threadbare pageant smile and tilted her head. "Things aren't always what they seem, Jane."

"Oh, I...I know that, Courtney."

Courtney sang along with Etta again. "Oh, yeah when you smile, you smile...Oh, and then the spell was cast..." A grim sadness suddenly fell hard over her. She leaned forward, speaking to the bartender. "Excuse me? Would you mind please turning this song down?" Her voice was anxious.

Jane turned to the bartender. "How about shutting it off?" She regarded Courtney. "That okay with you?"

Sweat beads formed along the rim of Courtney's lips. "Yes. Thank you."

The bartender turned off the music, leaving a stony silence in the place. Courtney took a generous gulp of her martini.

Jane gently spoke. "You know my story of why I started drinking…and I know yours."

"I should never have gone to those damn meetings!" Her visage became agitated as she let out a weary sigh. "But the judge told me that it was either that or jail for the DUI. And Craig was able to work his PR magic to make the public forget about my transgression. But spillin' my guts like I did at those meetings was *so wrong!*"

"Talking is always good. Hey, I had to learn that one too."

"Talk, talk, talk…What good did it do me?" She reached into her purse and removed an orange prescription bottle. "Nothing changed on the home front. If anything, it got worse." Popping the cap with her chipped thumbnail, she slid a tablet into her palm and then slammed it into her mouth, washing it down with the martini.

Jane couldn't help but see the name on the pill bottle. "Hey, I don't think you're supposed to mix alcohol with antidepressants."

Courtney tossed Jane a sarcastic smile. "Is that right?" She turned, staring straight ahead. Jane watched as Courtney momentarily detached from the scene and then re-entered her body. "Megan started preschool last year. But it hasn't been easy.… I've had *so* many calls from her teacher telling me that she wets the bed during naptime." She cleared her throat. "They suggested I take her to a child psychologist to find out what was bothering her. Well, I wasn't about to go down that rocky path. Can you imagine if her visits got out to people? And what would happen if she revealed something she shouldn't?" Courtney forced another tired smile, but this time it seemed harder to produce.

Jane knocked back her water. "You didn't need to take her to the doctor to find out why Megan was wetting the bed." She treaded cautiously. "You already knew the answer to that one."

Jane caught Courtney's reflection in the giant mirror behind the bar. She watched as Courtney's eyes narrowed, filling with pools of rage and sorrow. "Yes. I certainly *did*." Her voice was disincarnate. "But if it ever got out, Craig would find a way to spin it, wouldn't he?"

Jane wasn't sure Craig could "spin" that kind of sickness. Then again, it was painfully clear to Jane that Craig Gardner, up until now, had been able to skillfully strategize his sorry ass around any number of obstacles that might impede the progress of those who weren't initiated into the private manipulations of public relations. "I...," Jane hesitated briefly, "I offered to help you —"

Courtney suddenly came back into herself. "Oh, my goodness, Jane! Do you know what I suddenly flashed on right now? I've been having dreams about *you* for so many nights." She turned her body toward Jane. "Isn't that odd. Why would I be having dreams about *you*?"

Jane felt the knot tighten in her gut. "I don't know."

"I can't remember all of them...but..." Courtney closed her eyes. "Yes...I do recall you standing in front of me with your hand reaching out toward me." With her eyes still closed, she held out her hand, illustrating the pose. "And what was it you were saying in the dream to me? Oh, it's right there on the tip of my mind's eye; why can't I remember it?"

Jane checked the clock on the wall. 1:50. Ten minutes to closing time. She caught the eye of the bartender, who stared back at her with growing anxiety. Courtney opened her eyes. Jane quickly turned away from the bartender.

"Isn't that just the craziest thing, Jane?" Courtney nervously played with the sliver of lemon, bringing it to her lips and biting off a bit. But as she did it, the lemon slipped from her fingers and fell to the floor. "Oh, butterfingers!"

"Let me get it," Jane insisted. She slid off the stool and reached down to pick up the lemon. Her eyes rested on Courtney's left pant leg, which was tucked into the fur-trimmed white boots. A scarlet swath of fresh blood encircled the section of her pant leg right above the boot. Jane uneasily sat back onto the barstool. "Courtney? There's a lot of blood on your pant leg. Are you hurt?"

Courtney casually took a sip of her martini. "Are you sure?" she asked, never looking down. Jane nodded. "That's odd. I don't even feel it." She turned to the mirror that framed the bar. "You know what? I don't really feel anything."

Jane gingerly touched Courtney's sleeve. "Did Craig do that? Is that how this night started for you?"

An unnatural glaze washed over her countenance. "Oh, Jane. It doesn't matter. Really, honey…it doesn't matter…"

Jane pressed Courtney's sleeve to try to create a connection with her, but it was useless. "But it *does* matter, Courtney. Is that how it all started?"

Courtney turned to Jane, still distant but harboring a layer of agitation. "How *what* started, Jane?"

Jane stared at her. "Would you walk outside with me?"

A suspicious glower crept across her eyes. "Why?"

"I gotta get some air."

Courtney glanced down to the bar. "I'm sorry, Jane, but I can't go with you. I have other plans." She slid her right hand into her jacket pocket.

Jane heard the distinct *click* of a handgun being cocked. Her heart pounded. "Oh, fuck. Courtney, come on. What are you doing?"

Courtney tilted her head. An errant strand of hair fell across her cheek; she allowed it to linger on her moist skin. "Jane…Jane…Jane. I have no choice. I can't play the game any longer." She stopped, lost in thought. "My kids… my beautiful children — I know the son-of-a-bitch touched Megan. Not like he touches me. She gets the soft hand. I get the fist."

"I'll get you help," Jane urged. "You walk out of here with me, I'll get you help."

"Dear, dear, Jane…" Courtney twisted her hand in her jacket pocket to force the butt of the concealed gun into her gut. "You have no idea."

"No, Courtney, I *do*." She carefully slipped off the barstool and stood next to the bar. "Look, I've had a shitty night so far. I don't need to cap it off with you…capping yourself off."

Courtney momentarily looked blank, and then, as if a switch went off, she broke into uproarious laughter. "Oh, Jane! You enjoy such a humorous twist to the English language!"

Jane reached out toward her. "Please give me the gun, Courtney."

Courtney's laughter quickly ceased as a realization surfaced. "It's like the dream, Jane. Just now, you standing there like that, with your hand reaching toward me. Remember the dream I told you about? This here, *right now*, is it manifested in real life." She cocked her head. "Or is *this* a dream? I feel so very foggy, Jane." Courtney slid the revolver from her jacket pocket and, using the business end of the gun, itched her temple. The bartender could be heard slowly walking away in the background. "Huh…," she said, her eyes losing focus.

"What is it?" Jane carefully asked.

"I just realized that I don't remember how I got to this bar."

"Give me the gun, Courtney. Please?"

"How did I get here, Jane?"

"*Courtney!* Give me the gun."

Courtney disappeared into herself. "I drove," she muttered distantly. "How peculiar…"

"Please…give…me…the…gun," Jane pleaded.

Courtney stared at Jane, her eyes housing the specter of chaos. "Are you my friend, Jane?" She traced tiny circles in her cheek with the tip of the gun.

Jane let out a soft sigh. "Sure."

Courtney dove into Jane's eyes, searching for honesty. "I do believe you are being forthright with me, Jane Perry. Thank you." Courtney lowered the handgun but still held onto it. She regarded it for a moment as if she were seeing it for the first time. "My, my…" With that, Courtney quietly rested the gun on the bar.

Jane grabbed a napkin and, gingerly lifting the weapon, ejected the waiting bullet in the chamber and dumped the clip into her palm.

Courtney turned to the clock. "It's after two. The bartender left." Her voice was remote. "I guess we overstayed our welcome." She patted the perspiration from her forehead. "Is it hot in here to you, Jane?"

Jane felt her heart race as she placed the unloaded gun back onto the bar. "No, Courtney."

"Oh, it is to *me*." With that, she removed her jacket and plopped it onto the bar. Underneath, her petal pink turtleneck was covered with thick splatters of blood. Courtney let out a relieved breath. "Oh, *much* better!"

Jane drew Courtney's jacket toward her, placing it over the gun on the bar. "Courtney?" she said quietly.

Courtney's eyes drifted into another realm.

Jane moved her body so that she was in line with Courtney's gaze. "Courtney?" she repeated, this time with more urgency. Their eyes met. "You have to hear this. I processed a horrible crime scene tonight. The same one that Cynthia Taylor was reporting on the Channel 9 news? The one you saw on the TV when you came into this bar?" Courtney stared at Jane, nonplussed. "I found Craig in the living room. He was shot twice in the head and three times in the groin."

Courtney furrowed her brow. "No..."

"Megan was in her bed, shot once in the forehead. The two boys were in their beds, both shot once."

Courtney shook her head as her lip began to quiver. "What? It's a mistake...You are mistaken, Jane."

Jane felt herself breathing shallowly. "No, Courtney. I'm not mistaken." She weighed her words carefully. "It was graphic...and it was purposeful...."

Courtney looked off to the side. First there was no visible emotion and then a single tear emerged from her right eye, drifting awkwardly down her moist cheek and disappearing into the pink turtleneck. "I...," she paused, looking lost. "I couldn't leave the boys without a father or their sister. That wouldn't be right. So...I had no choice...." She turned to Jane. "They were asleep. So was Megan. Craig was awake though. I made damn sure of that. I wanted to make certain he saw *me*. I wanted him to understand what was about to happen. I told him that he would never hurt me again and that Megan would never get hurt again either."

"You didn't need to kill Megan."

"Oh, yes, I did." Courtney's voice was calm and blunt. "She was damaged goods. Just like I am. Who would love her, Jane? She was tainted by her own father.... I did what I did to her out of a mother's love."

Jane regarded Courtney with cautious disgust. "Courtney, I came to this bar tonight to arrest you. You have the right to remain silent. Anything you say or do can and will be held against you in the court of law...."

"Silent?" Courtney's voice rose several octaves. "I don't want to be silent, Jane! *Silence* is what got me where I am right now. I want to scream, Jane!" She flung her arms in the air, moving erratically around the bar. "I want everyone to know what happened to me...what happened to my daughter...."

Jane backed away from Courtney, giving the woman distance to vent. "You have the right to speak to an attorney," Jane pressed on. "If you cannot afford an attorney, one will be appointed for you —"

Courtney ambled closer to the bar, still waving her arms in the air. "I can afford the best goddamned attorney in the state of Colorado!"

Jane heard the click of the bar's front door opening and two sets of soft footsteps issuing forth. Courtney seemed unaware of the swift visitors. Jane needed to wrap things up here quickly. Pulling her handcuffs from her back pocket, she slowly walked toward Courtney. "Do you understand these rights as they have been read to you, Courtney?"

Courtney turned toward the bar, her back to Jane. "Oh, it's clear, honey!" She looked at the butt of her gun poking from underneath her jacket. "Deliriously clear!" Courtney grabbed the gun off the bar and swerved back around, arm outstretched toward Jane.

Jane instinctively reached for her Glock but screamed to the two others, now hidden in the folds of darkness. "*No!* Hold your fire!"

But her order and the deafening sound of 9-millimeter rounds merged. Two rounds punctured Courtney's already blood-splattered turtleneck and the third entered the side of her neck, slamming Courtney's body against the bar.

"Her gun isn't loaded!" Jane yelled. "*Her gun is not fucking loaded!*"

Two cops wearing heavy vests emerged from the darkened corner of the bar. One of them approached Jane. "She pointed a fucking gun at you! How in the hell are we supposed to know it's not loaded?!"

"Suicide by cop," the other officer mumbled.

Jane stared at Courtney. Her body slid from the bar onto the floor, her frail hand still clutching the toothless handgun. There was a sudden flutter of movement in her right eye. Jane quickly moved to Courtney. She knelt down beside her, cradling her head in one hand while pointlessly trying to stop the gush of blood from her neck with the other hand. A look of peace came over the dying woman as a thin smile crept across her pale, blood-laced face. She finally allowed the empty gun to slip from her hand. "Things aren't always what they seem, huh, Jane?" she stammered. As her eyes rolled back into her head, she whispered, "Lucky...lucky for me tonight..."

Courtney's death was called at 2:09 a.m. One by one, an onslaught of Denver PD reps and officers emerged from the shadows outside and filled the bar with their murmuring chatter. Jane stood back from the crush of suits and badges. Someone handed her a large cloth napkin to wipe Courtney's blood from her hand. She heard, "Sorry, Jane," and, "The woman gave us no choice," but their words fell like bricks.

Jane ducked outside the bar and stood under the crimson glare of Bloody Mary's neon sign. Lighting a cigarette, she took a deep drag, waiting for the nicotine to numb and grant her a few seconds of solitude. But the solitude never came. A gust of frosty wind brushed hard against Jane's body. She pulled her leather jacket tighter across her chest. The crunch of snow bit fangs of ice into her boots. A couple shots of Jack sounded so damn good at that moment. Yes, that would warm and soothe her twisting gut. But she was a recovering drunk, and she was standing there shivering outside of a bar after closing on a cold Denver night.

Things aren't always what they seem.

# A Note from the Author

Hello readers,

I wanted you to be the first to know that you're going to meet a new character soon that is not connected to Jane Perry.

Hold on! Before you get concerned that I'm ignoring Jane, rest assured that she will reappear in the summer of 2012 with the fourth book in her series. But before that, there's a new woman in town who I think will capture your heart.

Her name is Betty Craven. Like Jane, she lives in Colorado (although she hails from Texas). She doesn't solve crimes or talk like a sailor, but, she is tough. She has to be for what she experiences in her story.

Why did I create Betty Craven? Just like Jane Perry, Betty's character came to me from my own life experiences. While I am not Jane Perry, I am also not Betty Craven. However, both of these women and I share aspects that I think a lot of other women can relate to.

Over the last twelve months, I turned fifty, my mother died, and I witnessed a lot of people around me desperately fighting for what they thought was important to them. Some of those people lost everything, including their will to live. Others opted to completely transform themselves and bravely stepped outside their protective boxes and lived life from a new and much more honest perspective. Because they allowed their belief systems to change, they found an exhilarating freedom they'd never encountered. As I watched this profound transformation, I found a provocative sense welling up inside of me. A rebellion. A need to explore why I do what I do and think what I think.

I started asking myself the questions that I believe a lot of people start asking themselves when they realize they have more years behind them than in front of them. Am I happy? Are my belief systems based on my own reality or someone else's that I've blindly agreed to? Is life inherently tough or is it tough because you believe it has to be in order to succeed? Am I living my life too close to the vest? If so, is it time to rethink that? What are my greatest fears and how can I overcome them? These are only a few of the deep questions I posed to myself and ruminated on for quite some time.

And before long, Betty Craven was born. These themes and many others are featured in her story, which will probably be controversial to some readers who have fixed ideas. What Betty Craven does and why she does it, transforms her deeply and alters her life forever.

I hope that just as you have taken Jane Perry under your collective wings, you will also invite Betty Craven into your life. I know she's waiting to meet you.

Laurel Dewey

*Meet Betty when Laurel Dewey's new novel goes on sale from The Story Plant in early 2012.*

www.ingramcontent.com/pod-product-compliance
Lightning Source LLC
Chambersburg PA
CBHW010450100726
47904CB00008B/2550